THE
GIRL GUIDE
ANNUAL
1973

Published by special arrangement with
THE GIRL GUIDES ASSOCIATION

Illustrated by SHEILA CONNELLY

PURNELL
London, W.1

FEATHERY FREDDY

by Jean Kenward

Feathery Freddy
Lived up high
On the top of an ash-tree.
Wet or dry,
There he sat
Like the king of all,
Feathered and flashy
From tail to poll,
Mocking and squawking,
As if to say,
"I'm Feathery Freddy!
Look this way!"

At last the other birds
Upped and said,
"We wish that boastful
Fellow DEAD!
He breaks the nests,
He sucks the eggs;
He borrows and steals
And sneaks and begs.
Why don't he learn
BEHAVIOUR better?
Somebody ought
To send a letter."

They all cried "Yes!
Someone should write
To Feathery Fred
In black and white,
Telling him what
A nasty thing
He is with his endless
Posturing."
They wrote it once,
They wrote it twice,
Then tore it up,
Since it wasn't nice.

All those words
So cross and clever
Looked TERRIBLE when
They were put together,
And never a single
Bird would dare
To post such rudeness
Through the air.
Nobody did
And nobody will.
Feathery Freddy
Rocks there still.

THE GUIDE'S OWN ANNUAL

Front-cover photograph in colour of Guides of the 26th Cheltenham (St. Philip's) Company at the Rollright Stones, Oxfordshire

SBN 361 02020 1
Copyright © 1972 by PURNELL & SONS LTD.
Made and printed in Great Britain by
Purnell & Sons Ltd.
Paulton (Somerset) and London

A GUIDE FOR ALL SEASONS

by BARBARA BEACHAM

"Nothing ever happens in our Company," complained Nancy Phillips, rolling over on her back and closing her eyes. "It's so dull. The meetings lack swing and interest and—"

"It's only you, you know." Alison put the sticking-plaster in the small first-aid kit she always carried in her uniform pocket, and shut the lid. "There, that's done! Now for your problem, my child. You find our Company dull because you're not working hard at being a Guide."

Nancy's eyes flew open and she sat up indignantly. "I like that! Who came in first in the hundred-yards swim the other day? I reckon I worked jolly hard."

"*Then*, yes," agreed Alison. "But, honestly, Nan, when else and at what else have you really put yourself out?"

Nancy grinned. "All right, I'm lazy and uninterested and find Guides dull. What can I do about it?"

"Be a real Guide," urged Alison. "You'll soon find you're enjoying yourself, as well as learning lots. A Guide is for all seasons, you know—not just for camp or for Christmas—"

"Learning lots, you said. What for? What does

Nancy sat up sharply as Alison said: "You're not working at being a Guide"

it all lead to? Tell me that, Alison."

Alison stared at her. "Everything we learn at Guides teaches us, in a small way, how to cope with life. Didn't you know that?"

Nancy shook her head. "Perhaps I *had* better do something about it, then," she said lazily. "Tell me, how do I become a real Guide?"

"Oh, Nan, really!" Alison said, in exasperation. "What do the Law and the Promise say? Be honest with yourself and you'll know how to be a real Guide."

Nancy pulled a face. Picking up her school bag from where she had dumped it when they arrived back from Guides, she left her Leader and went home to tea. What she had said about the Guide Company had been only half true. Certainly she did not find the meetings very interesting, but she was honest enough to know that, as Alison said, it was partly her own fault.

She went to Guides to have a good time, to lark about and take nothing very seriously. It was a sort of light relief from her home life, and at first it was tremendous fun. Now, a year later, the interest was wearing thin.

A smell of cooking cabbage greeted her as she opened the front door, and she wrinkled her nose in disgust. Mrs. Watling had a one-track mind when it came to vegetables, and Nancy wondered her father didn't ask the housekeeper to cook something else sometimes. Mother used to cook all sorts of vegetables—peas, runner beans, parsnips.

Sudden tears filled Nancy's eyes, and a lump rose in her throat. Why did their family have to be different from everyone else's? She could remember other things about her mother more precious than the vegetables she cooked: the way her hair curled about her face, her happy laughter, and the feel of her encircling arms.

Nancy dropped her school bag on the floor with a bang.

"Nancy! Is that you?" Mrs. Watling's deep voice called from the kitchen. "Your dad's just phoned. His sister's had her baby. It's a girl. The twins are all over themselves thinking they've got a new playmate."

"Dad's not in, then?"

"No, and he isn't coming just yet. His sister's a bit low; she's worked herself to a standstill, what with the other two little 'uns to look after. Do her good to have a rest. Your dad's gone to see

"You little beasts!" cried Nancy furiously

her. Isn't it just like a man? Never mind his dinner
what's all ready for him! Hurry up now; it's on
the table. Call the twins, will you?"

Nancy sighed and went upstairs to the bedroom
she shared with her two small sisters. The day
before she had had a blitz on the room and cleaned
it up, put away all the twins' toys and clothes and
her own things too. She was pleased with the result,
and, thinking of her chat with Alison, she wondered whether her Leader would consider that the
job had been done in a Guide-like manner.

She opened the bedroom door, and then stopped
aghast. Tears of self-pity pricked her eyes. Both
small girls were there, the contents of their toy
cupboard strewn over the floor. But that was not
all. The cupboard itself lay on its side, and her
bed, stripped of all its clothes, was pushed under the
window. A drawer had been removed from the
chest in the corner and its contents spilled out on
her mattress. Becky was perched on the top of the
chest trying to hang a picture on the rail.

"What on earth!" Nancy could feel the anger
surging up in her, and she gave it full rein. "You
little beasts, what do you think you're doing?"

Belinda quailed before Nancy's wrath. "We—
we thought you'd like it," she said doubtfully.
"You always said you'd like your bed under the
window, so we—we put it there."

"You little idiots!" stormed Nancy. "It won't
fit there, not with all the other furniture. And look
at the mess you've made! Get down, Becky, and
get out!"

If there had been anywhere to sit she would
have sunk down and cried. All that work yesterday for nothing! Her tears began to flow, and she
pushed past Belinda to the corner where Becky was
lying on top of the chest with her legs over the
front searching for a foothold.

Nancy gave her a resounding slap. She knew it
had been Becky's idea; everything always was.
Belinda only followed. Becky's small face puckered,
but she did not cry, and Nancy, beside herself
with anger, picked her off the chest and dumped
her on the floor. "Get out!" she cried.

Becky stood her ground, her face red and her
hands clenched. "You're horrid," she cried, "and
we hate you, Belinda and me! One day we'll run
away, and you'll be sorry."

"Get out!" shouted Nancy. "Get out at once!"

The twins disappeared.

Nancy looked round the room. Where should she start? She had wanted to go to the swimming-baths after supper, when the twins were in bed, and now she wouldn't be able to. By the time she had cleared the room, the baths would be shut.

"Nancy!" Mrs. Watling's voice floated up the stairs. "Come on!"

Rubbing her hand quickly across her eyes, Nancy went to the door. A crunch under her foot made her look down. On the floor lay her Guide badge, the pin broken from the back.

That was the last straw. Slamming the door, she stamped downstairs and marched into the kitchen.

"Whatever's going on?" demanded Mrs. Watling, coming to the scullery door.

"Ask those little beasts," stormed Nancy, her face red with anger. "And take a look at the bedroom. I'm going out."

She strode to the door, grabbed her swimsuit

Under her foot lay a Guide badge, broken

and towel, which were lying in the hall, and ran down the path, leaving the chaos behind.

The heat of her anger wore itself out in the swimming-baths. Nancy took stock of the situation as she towelled herself dry and dressed. She was ravenously hungry, but had no money to buy food, having spent her last cash to get into the baths. It was still on the early side to go home; the twins wouldn't be in bed yet, as Mrs. Watling would have to put the room to rights first.

She rolled up her wet costume in the damp towel, put her Guide uniform back on, and opened the door of the bathing cubicle.

"Worked it off?" asked a voice.

Nancy spun round. "Alison!"

Alison laughed. "I'm glad you've seen me at last. You look like a thundercloud. What's up?"

Nancy's lips tightened. "Oh, I don't know—everything!"

"Well, let's see if we can sort something out on the way home. I've got my bike. Have you?"

"No; I walked."

"Well, I'll walk as far as your house with you."

Nancy knew that her Leader did not really understand her problem, for Alison's home life was quite different from hers. All the same, Nancy had a great respect for Alison, as well as liking her. Alison wore an armful of badges on her uniform, and she always worked hard at Guides, yet was never swanky about her achievements. Yes, she was a very useful person to have around.

As they neared Nancy's home, the two girls saw Mrs. Watling at the gate, looking up and down the road.

"I'm glad you've come back just now, Nancy," Mrs. Watling said. "The twins are not in the garden, and it's past their bedtime. I wondered if they'd gone to meet you."

"No, they haven't," said Nancy, with a sigh. "I suppose they're hiding somewhere. I'll look for them."

She and Alison hunted everywhere they could think of, looking in all the twins' favourite hiding-places, but the two children were not to be found. Alison suggested they might have gone to a friend's house, but when Nancy checked up no one had seen them.

"You'd best cycle round the streets," said Mrs. Watling at last.

"All right," said Nancy. "I'll get my bike."

A fear was beginning to worry her that the twins were not hiding. Had they forgotten the time, or, because of her unkindness to them earlier in the evening, had they done what Becky had said they would do one day, and run away?

"It's a child's toy," said Alison, turning something over with her foot

When Nancy found that the twins' bicycles were not in the shed, the half-formed fear took root, and she raced back to the house.

"Their bikes have gone! I think—I think they've run away!"

"Run away!" said Mrs. Watling, sitting down suddenly. "Well, I suppose it's not surprising, the way you treated them, Nancy—them with no mother an' all."

Nancy's face flooded with colour, and Alison said quickly, "Let's go up to their room and see if they've taken anything else besides their bikes."

The bedroom was tidy now. Becky's koala bear and Belinda's teddy bear, with the twins' blue hair-ribbons round their necks, were in their usual places on the beds. All the twins' clothes were in the cupboard and drawers.

"No," said Alison. "If everything's here, they won't have run away."

Nancy went to the window and looked out into the garden, her back to Alison. She didn't want her Leader to see the tears of thankfulness in her eyes. The twins had probably cycled to the park and didn't realise how late it was, the evenings being long and light. They hadn't run away because she'd been horrible to them.

Nancy caught her breath. There on the window-sill, behind the curtain, was the twins' piggy-bank, broken open and empty of money.

Nancy's face was chalk-white as she turned to Alison. "Why would they take all their money? They *have* run away," she whispered. "They've taken all their money."

Alison put her arm round her. "We'll go after them. Have you any idea where they would go? You think while I get Mrs. Watling to phone the police."

She piloted Nancy down the stairs and ran out into the kitchen. By the time Mrs. Watling had taken in all that was required of her, Nancy had recovered a little and was waiting at the gate.

"I can't seem to think straight," she said as Alison came down the path. "Where would they go? Where shall we start to look for them?"

"If they've run away," said Alison, "I expect they'll steer clear of the town and go somewhere into the country."

The road where Nancy lived was long and straight and led from the town into the country. The girls cycled fast to the end of the road, where they had a choice of turning right or left. Alison braked to a stop. Jumping off her bike, she crossed the road by a zebra crossing. She paused on the far pavement and turned something over in the gutter with her foot.

"What's that?" asked Nancy.

"It's a child's toy. It looks like a monkey," said Alison.

Nancy was off her bike and across the road in a flash. "It's Becky's," she cried, picking it up and

"Look—tyre-marks!"

turning it over in her hands. "She had it in her bicycle basket."

"It probably fell off as she bumped her bike up the pavement," said Alison. "Good! That means they came this way."

They set off again. If only she hadn't been so cross with the twins, thought Nancy, none of this need have happened. Where were they? What were they doing? Were they all right? Suddenly Nancy knew how much she loved her little sisters, in spite of their tiresome ways, and how much she longed to know they were safe.

The road they were on began to narrow; the houses and pavements stopped, and the girls cycled between hedges ablaze with wild roses and honeysuckle. Nancy did not see the flowers. She was trying to imagine where her sisters were going, for this road led right into the country.

They spun down a steep hill and splashed through a small stream that ran across the road. Alison pulled up so abruptly the other side that Nancy almost came off her bike.

"Sorry!" said Alison, staring at the ground. "I was thinking that if they came this way we'd see their tyre-marks from the stream. Yes, look, there they are!"

Then her expression became grave. Nancy knew in an instant why.

"Alison, the quarry!" They turned along the track to the quarry.

Alison nodded. "Come on!" she murmured. "Hurry!"

Nancy needed no urging. The track to the quarry was rough. They tore along it. Both girls became bruised as the bumps and hollows flung them up and down in the saddles.

At the end of the track, on a level patch of grass, lay the twins' bicycles. White-faced, Nancy flung herself from her machine and raced to the edge of the plateau. She could scarcely steel herself to look over. The quarry was deep and dangerous. Its sides sloped gently for a short distance, but they were covered with layers of loose stones that needed only a slight impulsion to set off a minor avalanche. Beyond the gentle slope was a precipitous cliff that dropped sheer to the quarry floor.

Gazing over, Nancy felt her blood run cold. The twins were there, both of them—on the last dip of the slope, within yards of the precipice.

Both were clearly paralysed with fright, crouched on the shifting stones that at a movement could send them sliding over the edge and into the quarry eighty feet below.

Belinda heard the girls, and turned her white face to them. Becky was a yard or more nearer the edge. Nancy could guess what had happened. Becky, the bold, venturesome one, had gone down the slope and set the stones moving; she'd been carried almost to the lip of the drop and dared not move for fear of being carried over. Belinda had probably gone to help her and become trapped as well on a layer of treacherous stones.

"Don't move! I'm coming!" cried Nancy, and began to descend the slope.

"No, you're not!" Alison grabbed her arm and held it firmly.

"Let me go!" shouted Nancy, struggling angrily to free herself.

"Stay where you are!" snapped Alison. "Once you're on those stones you'll be as helpless as they are. We need a rope, and there is one—a skipping-rope. I spotted it in one of the twins' bike baskets as we came by. It may make just the difference between reaching them and not. Hang on!"

Nancy's resistance collapsed. She thanked heaven silently for Alison. The P.L. had kept her head. Alert, she had spotted the skipping-rope in one of the bike baskets. Calm, unpanicked in the face of an urgent, desperate crisis, with two young lives literally hanging in the balance, she had quietly, coolly, assessed the situation and devised the best way to set about a rescue without waste of time.

"Take one end of the skipping-rope." Alison was back. She thrust the wooden handle of Belinda's skipping-rope into Nancy's hand. "Go down the slope as gently as you can. Remember that even a slight movement starts the stones moving. I'll hold on to the other end of the rope. It may not be long enough for us to reach Belinda without getting on to the stones, but it'll give us some extra distance."

Alison had wasted no time in superfluous argument. Although she was lighter than Nancy, she knew it would be useless to suggest going first, and seconds were too precious to waste in futile debate.

Nancy clutched the skipping-rope handle, and carefully, gingerly, descended the slope. She was

soon on the stones, which moved treacherously under her feet; but the rope, firmly held by Alison, steadied her and kept her from starting an avalanche.

Step by step, she went down. With the skipping-rope at full stretch and Alison only just on the beginning of the stones, she was able to reach Belinda.

"Give me your hand, Belinda," she breathed out.

With her own arm outstretched to its fullest extent, she was able to grasp Belinda's hand in hers.

"Hang on!" she called back to Alison. "I'm going to pull Belinda now."

Alison held firmly on to the rope. The stones moved ominously as Belinda stepped past Nancy and grabbed the rope, but only a few on the top

Step by step Nancy went down the treacherous slope

She clung to the rope as the stones swept down

ward rush into the quarry—and there was only a narrow margin between her and the edge.

Holding fiercely on to the taut rope, she pulled Becky slowly to her. Very gingerly, she turned, still clutching Becky, to go back up the slope. As she did so, the stones began to move. A slide began. At first a trickle, it quickly became a flood. Nancy's feet slid from under her. She cried out. Then through the cloud of dust thrown up by the sliding stones, she saw Alison, and suddenly realised that all was well; she was firmly held.

Alison had her free hand firmly anchored in a hole in the slope while her other hand kept a tenacious grip on the skipping-rope. The hole might have been a rabbit's or a fox's or any other creature's, but whatever it was Alison had found it and, like the quick-thinking, resourceful, trained Guide that she was, seen its value and utilised it.

The stones swept over the quarry edge in a hideous tide, but Nancy clung on to the rope with one hand and held Becky with the other, and when the avalanche subsided she was able to climb slowly up the rope to Alison.

The worst was over. The rope, with Alison anchored on the other end, had saved her and Becky from disaster. They had to exercise great care in ascending the upper part of the slope, but as soon as their feet were clear of the treacherous stones they felt safe.

At the top, Nancy put her arms round the twins and hugged them.

"We only wanted flowers for Aunty Muriel and the baby," sobbed Belinda. "The shops were shut, so we couldn't buy the rattle."

"We saw the flowers down there, and we thought they'd be nice for Aunty Muriel," said Becky.

"Then Becky slipped and couldn't get back, and I tried to help her and couldn't get back, either."

Nancy looked at Alison, and Alison smiled back at her. Nancy couldn't speak. She wanted to and tried to, but couldn't.

"You've got a very brave sister," Alison told the twins. "She loves you so much she risked her life for you."

"Who's talking?" cried Nancy, tongue suddenly loosened. "I'll tell you something else, Becky and Belinda. If it hadn't been for Alison, none of us would be here now. She's a real Guide, and that's why you were rescued and I was saved from going over into the quarry. Alison's a Guide the whole Company is proud of, a proper Guide—and that's what I'm going to try to be from now on—a Guide like Alison, a real Guide; what was it you said, Alison?—a Guide for all seasons."

went rolling down and over the edge. Alison reached out and caught Belinda, who crawled past her and then safely up on to the grassy part of the slope.

"Now for Becky!" muttered Nancy.

Her heart was in her mouth as she moved, half slithering, downwards. Becky was perilously near the edge of the quarry, and one false move might send all three of them over in an avalanche of stones.

Nancy dared not look back at Alison, who she knew must now be wholly on the shifting stones.

"I'm coming, Becky dear—don't be afraid!" she breathed.

Becky's lips were pressed together in a tight line. She was obviously terrified. She didn't speak, but her head turned ever so slightly as Nancy's hand reached out to her. She clutched at the hand and gripped it desperately.

Nancy could now see into the quarry, and her blood ran cold. She knew it was touch-and-go. The stones were so loose that even the act of turning to go back up the slope could start them on a down-

WIN A SUPERB
CASSETTE RECORDER AND £50!

A superb cassette recorder of the latest type, worth £50, plus £50 for your Company to spend on camping or other Guiding equipment – that's the exciting double prize that could be yours in this interesting and simple competition. Instead of the recorder, you could choose something else of equivalent value, if you wished.

When you have read your *Girl Guide Annual*, choose what you think is the best and next best story, article, etc. in each of the six groups printed below, then say in not more than about fifty words what you like most about the *Girl Guide Annual*.

The double prize will be awarded to the entry that exactly or most nearly agrees with the one the Editor has marked up and that has the most interesting write-up.

GROUP 1 (STORIES)
A   A Guide for All Seasons
B   Jumble Luck
C   The Strange Affair at Four Oaks
D   The Cantankerous Old Harridan
E   Catch Me a Woodpecker
F   The Two-Treasures Hunt

GROUP 2 (PUZZLES)
A   Cookery Puzzle
B   ABC Stairs
C   The Crafty Kingfishers
D   Which Patrol Bird?
E   What's the Message?
F   Which Patrols?
G   Pick the Flowers

GROUP 3 (MAKING, GROWING)
A   Pottery-Making
B   "Our Chalet" Pop-Up
C   Rope Models
D   How to Grow Herbs
E   Make a Tree-Board
F   Friezes for Fun
G   Red Indian Notice-Board
H   Camp and Corner Tidy
I   Preserve Spring Flowers
J   Camp Fridge
K   "Seasons of the Year" Presents
L   Fun with Wood
M   The 24-Hour Clock

GROUP 4 (FOR BADGES)
A   Seeing Stars
B   Feather Finding
C   Don't Get Tied Up in Knots

GROUP 5 (POEMS)
A   Feathery Freddy
B   Ask a Guide
C   Thinking Day
D   Moss
E   Camp Hazards
F   The Moth
G   Wily Whip Weasel

GROUP 6 (ARTICLES)
A   "Our Chalet"
B   "Be Prepared"
C   Letter to Jane
D   Guide Laws
E   Once a Guide. . . .
F   Gracious Guiding
G   Girls in the Gang Show
H   The Slim and Svelte Patrol
I   Do Guides Lack Humour?
J   Gillian on Safari

- -

THE GIRL GUIDE ANNUAL NEW COMPETITION ENTRY FORM

Just write down the letter that is set against the title of your choice in the list above

GROUP 1 (STORIES)
BEST   D
NEXT BEST   A

GROUP 2 (PUZZLES)
BEST   F
NEXT BEST   B

GROUP 3 (MAKING, GROWING)
BEST   L
NEXT BEST   E

GROUP 4 (FOR BADGES)
BEST   C
NEXT BEST   F

GROUP 5 (POEMS)
BEST   E
NEXT BEST   B

GROUP 6 (ARTICLES)
BEST   C
NEXT BEST   J

MY NAME AND ADDRESS: Gillian Lockhart, 125 High St, bonnybridge, stirlingshire, Scotland

MY AGE: 10   MY COMPANY: 3rd Bonnybridge

MY GUIDER'S NAME AND ADDRESS: Mrs Davies

THE GIRL GUIDE ANNUAL
EXCITING NEW £100 PRIZE COMPETITION

So successful was the double-prize competition in last year's *Girl Guide Annual* that the publishers are inviting you to enter another one this year.

The competition gives an equal chance to every Guide, regardless of age.

Not only can you win the prize of a really fine cassette recorder with all the latest refinements, but you can win £50 for your Company at the same time! Incidentally, instead of the recorder, you can choose a bicycle, a transistor radio, a fully automatic camera, a record player, or something else of equivalent value.

Don't rush to enter! Read and enjoy your *Girl Guide Annual* at leisure. Then, when you have decided which of the various contributions in each group printed overleaf you like best and next best, fill in the entry form and then write briefly and to the point in the space below what you like most about the *Girl Guide Annual*.

When you have completed both front and back of the entry form, cut it out and put it, unfolded, in an envelope addressed to THE GIRL GUIDE ANNUAL NEW COMPETITION, PURNELL/BANCROFT BOOKS, 49/50 POLAND STREET, LONDON, W.1.

Your entry must arrive not later than March 31st, 1973. The result will be published in *Today's Guide* in the last week of June, 1973.

The publishers' decision is final, and no correspondence will be entered into in connection with the competition.

What I like most about the Girl Guide Annual

I like the way it is set out with exiting storys and storyes for all kinds of people It tells you a lot about Guides and also has educational Puzzles the articles are really good and some of the Jokes are side spliting on the Whole the book is great!

30
40
&3

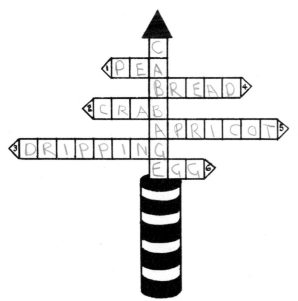

COOKERY PUZZLE

by M. I. ECKHARDT

If you answer the clues correctly the word down will spell something a Guide will eat but must never become.

1. In a shooter or a pod
2. Apple or shellfish
3. Wet or fat
4. Toast it or butter it
5. Can it or stew it, but eat it
6. Hen fruit

ANSWERS
6. Egg
5. Apricot
4. Bread
3. Dripping
2. Crab
1. Pea

WORD DOWN: Cabbage.

WALK DOWN THE A, B, C STAIRS

Fill in the blank squares from these clues.

A. An insect very much like an aunt.
B. A pig but not a bore.
C. Wading bird that doesn't lift weights.
D. He's not an ass.
E. Insects Guides don't like in their tent.
F. A flower for a well-dressed fox.
G. Could be described as a green plum.
H. Border of perennial flowers.

ANSWERS
H. Herbaceous
G. Greengage
F. Foxglove
E. Earwigs
D. Donkey
C. Crane
B. Boar
A. Ant

— DODSWORTH. —

"Keep still a second, Jennifer!"

Pottery-Making at Home

Try It If You Are Exploring the Arts

Suggests TREVOR HOLLOWAY

Pottery-making is one of the oldest crafts and one of the most fascinating. There is something thrilling in making an article direct from the raw materials right through to the finished product.

If you are unable to attend evening classes at which pottery-making is taught, don't despair—a wide range of small pottery can be made at home without the need for expensive equipment. You can even cope with firing and glazing.

A few Guides may be fortunate in having clay in their gardens. The rest can either obtain supplies through a craft shop (it is available in a variety of colours such as white, buff, terra-cotta, etc.) or from a local pottery or brickworks.

Garden clay needs to be thoroughly cleaned before it is fit for use. Break it into small pieces, mix with water until it has the consistency of thick cream, then sieve through a double thickness of butter-muslin into a bucket. Allow the liquid (known as "slip") to settle, then drain off the surplus water. Place the bucket of slip in the sun, or in a warm place, and leave until it is stiff enough to handle. All clays must be thoroughly kneaded before use.

Now to experiment! A simple thumb pot, such as made by potters in very early times, is a good type for the beginner. Take a lump of well-kneaded clay and roll it into a ball a little smaller than, say, a tennis-ball. Hold the clay ball in the palm of your right hand, press your left thumb into the centre of the clay and begin working the ball round and round, shaping the wall of the pot between your thumb and finger-tips. Gradually the height of your pot will increase and the wall become thinner. You could make the pot cup-like in shape, or taper it in towards the top like a goblet.

To make a neat base, roll out a "worm" of clay, then join the ends to make a circle of appropriate diameter. Weld the clay ring to the underside of the pot, pressing it firmly in place.

Decoration could be added in a number of ways. Indented designs could be made with such things as pencils, door keys, etc.; or you could make, say, a leaf-shape or a trefoil from a separate piece of clay and press it firmly on to the side of your pot.

Before venturing to fire a piece of pottery, you may like to get in a little more practice at shaping the clay first, so why not try your hand at a coil pot? Flatten a small ball of clay into a disc about $\frac{1}{4}$-inch thick. Now roll out "worms" of clay, form them into circles, and proceed to build up the wall of your pot by

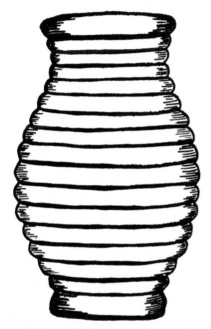

A coil pot is built up from rings of clay pressed firmly on top of each other

placing one circle firmly on top of another. Gradually increase or decrease the diameter of the rings according to the shape of pot you fancy. By the way, it is a good idea to lay the clay rings in place in such a way that the joins are staggered—then they won't be so obvious.

To give a decorative appearance, some of the rings could be flattened out to make a smooth surface—say, a smooth band near the base of the pot and another near the top.

Biscuit Firing

First, a *must!* Articles for firing must be *absolutely dry*, otherwise the heat will shatter them to ruins!

Carefully place your handiwork in a clean tin (such as a toffee canister or a large treacle-type tin without lids). Stand this tin in an empty fire-grate, then over this tin place a second and slightly larger tin so that there is a space between the inner and outer tins. The inner tin should have a few holes pierced in it to allow any moisture to escape freely.

Now build a fire around the tins and keep them covered by red-hot coals all day. Allow the fire to die down as usual at night and carefully remove the tins from the cold ashes in the morning. The tins, of course, will be useless, but with average luck your first piece of fired pottery will be safe and sound. This first firing is known as "biscuit" firing.

Glaze Firing

A biscuit-fired article, though hard, is porous like a flower-pot and if filled with

A thumb pot is shaped from a ball of clay

Biscuit Firing: Build your fire around the tins
A—OUTER TIN   B—INNER TIN   C—VENT HOLES IN INNER TIN

water and used as a flower-vase it would very soon show signs of leakage. To render it waterproof and to give it a pleasing finish, the work must be glazed. Here are two "recipes" which are simple and cheap.

Well mix with water into a thick cream 2 parts of dry powdered clay, 1 part of lime carbonate (whiting), and 10 parts of waterglass egg-preserver (these last two items can be obtained from your chemist). By the way, different coloured clays will give different coloured glazes.

The second method is even simpler: mix 4 parts of powdered clay and 5 parts of borax with water to make a thick cream.

The glaze should be applied very thickly, and the work is then fired in exactly the same way as described for biscuit firing.

Apart from proving a fascinating hobby, home-made pottery could also help to swell Patrol or Company funds.

ASK A GUIDE

by Judith E. Harrison

1st Dolphinholme Company, near Lancaster
who wrote this poem for the Writer Badge

I am a Girl Guide dressed in blue;
A very good turn I'll do for you.
If you are sick I'll wash your pots,
Do the shopping, mend your socks.
I don't mind how hard the work,
For dirty jobs I'll never shirk,
So just remember when distressed
Ask a Guide—she'll do her best.

"Our Chalet"

How a Dream Came True   by Alix Liddell

"I should like to give that house," said Mrs. Storrow, "and I should like it to be in Switzerland"

The members of the World Committee meeting in the Netherlands in 1929 had no idea that the stoutish, middle-aged American Girl Scout Leader occupying the Chair was no less a person than a fairy godmother in disguise—but that was what she turned out to be.

How to form a single united sisterhood of the Guides and Girl Scouts in the different countries of the world was the question under discussion. Somebody said, "What we need is a sort of international Foxlease, a house not belonging to any particular country but one which every Guide would think of as her very own."

There was a sigh as everyone contemplated this "castle in Spain", for the year-old World Association had very little money.

Then the fairy godmother revealed herself. "I should like to give that house," said Mrs. Storrow, "and I should like it to be in Switzerland."

It seemed only a matter of moments before Helen Storrow, accompanied by Dame Katharine Furse and a Swiss Guider best known as "Falk", were tramping over mountains and valleys looking for a suitable building to turn into a Guide home.

"If you should feel hungry at any time," said Dame Katharine to her Swiss companion, "don't hesitate to mention the fact, otherwise Aunt Helen will certainly not stop for anything so trivial as a meal."

None of the houses they inspected seemed quite the thing, but the fairy godmother was undismayed. "We shall just have to build one," she said. "Now it only remains to find the perfect spot." But that proved equally difficult.

Then one day they came to a plot of ground overlooking Lake Thun. "Here," said Mrs. Storrow, "one can find peace for the soul."

But Falk, thinking of the young people who would come there, considered it too tame. Ski-ing and climbing, she reckoned, would be more in their line, but Aunt Helen had fallen in love with this spot, and that apparently was that.

One day in the summer of 1930 Falk, at home in Berne, received a command: "Get ready to fly with me to England tomorrow. I want you to come to the World Conference at Foxlease and tell them about our plans."

The delegates at Foxlease were ecstatic over Aunt Helen's photographs and seemed uninterested in Falk's theory that "peace for the soul" was not what young people required.

Then the Founder himself spoke, with the well-known twinkle in his eye. "Well, Falk, if you don't approve of this place you will just have to find another!"

Mrs. Storrow was perfectly content to accept his decision, and so the hunt began again.

Some months later Falk rushed into Guide headquarters in Berne. "I have found the perfect spot!" she cried, expecting everybody to leap up with shouts of joy. Her words caused hardly a stir. Apparently, it was the twentieth time she had made such an announcement—but this time it was true.

Under the inspired direction of Mr. de Sinner, the architect entrusted with the task of transforming the "castle in Spain" into "Our Chalet in Switzerland", the building began to take shape, rising from a grassy alpine pasture across the valley from the village of Adelboden.

Six weeks before the official opening, planned for July, 1932, Mrs. Storrow appeared on the scene. She was delighted with all she saw. "And now," she said to the architect, "I want a miniature chalet for my personal use, and of course it must be finished in time for the opening."

Mr. de Sinner took it in his stride, and the baby chalet was all complete on the great day—two bedrooms, two bathrooms and a sitting-room.

What a great day that was! The Founder was there with his wife, the World Chief Guide; Dame Katharine and members of the World Committee; Guide Leaders from far away; near neighbours from Adelboden; and, of course, the fairy godmother and Falk, proud and happy that the dream had come true.

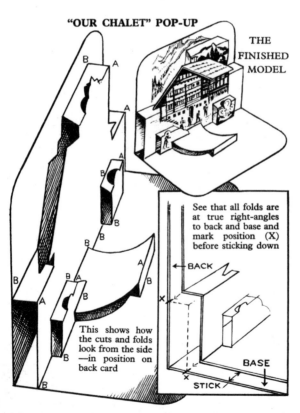

"OUR CHALET" POP-UP

THE FINISHED MODEL

See that all folds are at true right-angles to back and base and mark position (X) before sticking down

← BACK

This shows how the cuts and folds look from the side —in position on back card

BASE

STICK

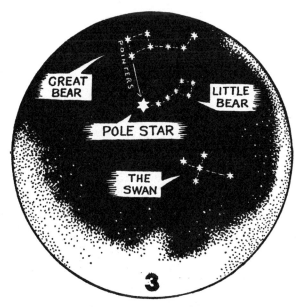

Autumn: November, 8.0 p.m.
Note the Pointers of the Great Bear; they point to the Pole Star

stars in the Great Bear have two front stars which are called "pointers". The distance between these two "pointers" multiplied by five gives the approximate distance from them to the Pole Star to which they point.

An easy way to identify three constellations in all the seasons of the year is to cut out a circle of cardboard about the size of a dinner-plate. Paint this dark-blue with poster paint, and cut twenty stars out of silver paper, making one slightly larger than the others. With hinges such as are used for stamp collections, stick the silver stars onto the blue cardboard to make the three constellations of your choice, using the largest piece of silver paper as the Pole Star.

As the seasons change you can move the "constellations" on your "sky" to match the movements of the constellations in the real sky.

to be in the same place. This is the North or Pole Star, which stands almost directly above Earth's North Pole, and is therefore due north at all times. It is easy to identify the Pole Star because of the Great Bear constellation. The seven bright

Try doing this by going out and looking at the stars, but to help you start there are four pictures here which show the three constellations called the Great Bear, the Little Bear and the Swan, as well as the Pole Star. Notice how these constellations are in different positions in the sky in different seasons of the year.

Badge Requirements

When you can easily recognise these three constellations, try making others on your cardboard sky. For the Star Gazer badge you have to be able to point out at least four constellations visible all the year round, four not visible throughout the year, and the constellations to which four stars of the first magnitude belong. You have to keep a log too, and demonstrate the position of heavenly bodies.

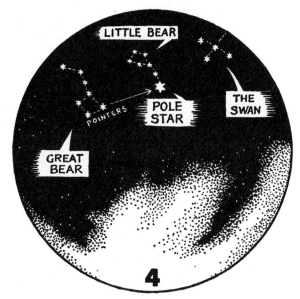

Winter: February, 8.0 p.m.

OPERATION MOUNTAIN-TOP

A GUIDE ADVENTURE STORY IN PICTURES by Rikki Taylor

THE NARROW TRACK ALONG THE QUARRY FACE THAT KIM HAD FOLLOWED PETERED OUT, AND THE BIG PUPPY COULDN'T GO ON OR BACK

29

THE GUIDES REPORTED THEIR DISCOVERY TO THE LOCAL POLICE

AT THE NEXT COMPANY MEETING, THE GUIDER SPOKE ABOUT THE RAVENS' MOUNTAIN-TOP OPERATION

Rope Models

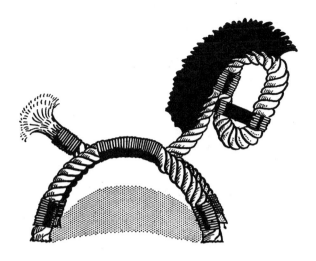

by Rex Hazlewood

In Switzerland I noticed some most attractive models of horses and riders and all sorts of other things made out of rope and selling at a very high price! Here, we thought, is an idea for Guide funds.

First of all, you must be sure you know how to whip a rope. Refresh your memory.

A Rope Horse

For a rope horse you will require rope cut into three parts: two five-inch lengths for the legs; the other length for the rest of the horse. Now take some florist's wire; insert in one of the shorter pieces of rope and, holding the rope in the left hand and the wire in the right, let the wire slip into the grooves of the rope, turning gently but firmly as you do this. Cut off the unrequired end of the wire and whip each end of the rope LEG about half an inch from each end with red twine. Repeat this operation with the other LEG. They will now  be stiffish and will bend into two curving shapes. Now wire up the long piece of rope.

Next whip one end of the long piece of rope with red twine; take the opposite end and twist it up and back to meet again, then whip firmly; now bind the lower end by the mouth more loosely. Place the two LEGS exactly opposite on either side of the body length. Whip very firmly over and over, and also cross-wise—under the tail and round the throat—until firmly fixed. Now take some light-brown wool—fold it over and over again on a piece of card that is about two inches wide and three inches long. After about three thicknesses of wool have been wound, work chain-stitch all down the ridge, taking up all the wool.

Cut up the opposite ridge of the card, and you will have the horse's mane. Sew it to the rope so that it hangs over the top of the HEAD, giving the impression of having ears. Fan out the rope-end for the tail so that it is nice and bushy.

A Rope Guide

Follow the same principles as set forth in part one with wiring the rope and whipping the ends. Cut three pieces of rope, as follows : Body a seven-inch length, wired and whipped each end ; arms a six-inch length, wired and whipped each end. Be sure to make a neat job of it.

Take the body length, and bend it at the hips, leaving one inch the other end for the neck. Pass the legs through the bend and bind them on firmly with twine.

Next put the arms in place at the base of the neck and bind on with twine, if possible giving the effect of a Guide tie. The head might be a table-tennis ball glued on to the neck, or you might prefer to use a wooden ball with a hole bored in it for the neck to be inserted. The features of course will be drawn or painted on.

For the overblouse and skirt wind round pale-blue and navy-blue wool. Stick on wool for plaits.

The Guide cap is made of stout paper. A dab of glue will hold it in position.

31

CAMP COMPETITIONS

Suggestions from ANNE ROBERTSON

When our Guide Company goes off each year to camp, one of the first things our Guider does is to tell us all about the competition which will run throughout the week. The members of each Patrol work together on all parts of the competition, and coloured tapes are awarded for first, second and third places. We fix these tapes to our Patrol totem poles, and on the last day of the week the winning Patrol is given the camp trophy.

Here are some suggestions for your own camp competition. You will probably be able to think of many more.

1. Make a gadget, using only branches and string, to hold a basin, soap and towel.
2. Plan a menu for a camp meal (two courses), using only one pan.
3. Design and make a Patrol totem pole.
4. Draw a scale map of the route from camp to the nearest town or village.
5. Measure the speed of the nearest river or stream.
6. Make a device for telling the time.
7. Light a fire in the middle of a stream and boil half a pint of water.
8. Compose a song for this camp.
9. Make a shelter or tree-house, using only natural materials.
10. Make a viewfinder to show landmarks seen from the top of the nearest hill.

Of course, you would not manage to do all these in a week! Six items would probably be enough, as your spare time will be limited. You will have lots of fun doing them, however, even if you don't win the trophy!

NATURE LORE

WHAT IS A SKIP JACK?

Another name for it is click beetle. Brown in colour, three-quarters of an inch in length, it is often found in the garden and attacks many of our garden flowers. When it falls on its back it uses a powerful muscle under its "waist" and its wing-cases as a spring and with a sudden jerk leaps into the air. It continues to do this until it falls right way up and can crawl out of sight. It would be a certain choice for the beetle Olympics! The young beetle grubs are known as wireworms. What a horrible name!

WHAT IS A SILVER FISH?

Yes, it is an award in Guiding, but the one that is the subject of this question is one of a curious family of insects known as bristle-tails. It is silvery-white in colour and covered in scales; hence its "fishy" name. You may even have some in your home, because they thrive in pantries, kitchens, storehouses and places like bakeries where sugary and starchy foods are kept. It measures from a third to three-quarters of an inch in length. Several of its country cousins live under stones, fallen leaves and tree-bark.

THINKING DAY

by Marcia M. Armitage

On this special day all over the world
The flags of Guiding are being unfurled.
All in our own way we pray,
Joined by the bond of Thinking Day.
Australia, India, Denmark, Japan,
Join in the fellowship Britain began.
America, Canada, France and Korea—
This day in February brings them all near.
In lands far and wide we have friends by the score,
And as each year comes we shall gain more and more.
With so much goodwill surely troubles should cease
And Guiding bring into this world love and peace.
So not just today should we think of our friends;
Let the Thinking Day spirit go on without end.

33

HOW TO GROW HERBS AND USE THEM

A. BABINGTON TELLS YOU

A herb garden is very easy to make, and provides interest when it is growing. Although we do not use herbs in large quantities, as our ancestors did, they can still be very useful when you cook.

Only a small piece of garden is required for herbs. An old stone sink or a window-box could be used instead of a portion of garden. I once saw a very original herb garden made in an old cartwheel, a different herb growing in each section of the wheel!

Here is a selection of the most popular and useful herbs to grow.

PARSLEY. The seed can be sown in early spring. It is slow to germinate, so do not lose patience! Some people sow the seed with radish to act as a "marker" crop.

MINT. The roots spread easily, so it is a good idea to plant it in an open polythene bag sunk into the soil.

CHIVE. This has a mild onion flavour. Plant the onion-like bulbs six inches apart, then cut regularly when the grass-like stalks appear.

SAGE. Buy a root or beg a cutting from a friend. It is a perennial. The leaves are used mainly in stuffings.

THYME. This is strongly flavoured, so use with care. Plant a root or cutting. The leaves are small, and the plant itself is an evergreen.

BAY. Another strongly flavoured leaf, dark and glossy. When crushed it has a penetrating aroma. Plant a root or cutting.

Now here are some suggestions for using the herbs in cooking. They can be used fresh, when they have more flavour. Try small quantities at first until you are accustomed to the flavour. The exception to this is parsley, which has a mild, pleasing taste.

Parsley Fish Cakes: Small tin of tuna or pink salmon. Three cooked potatoes. Tablespoon chopped parsley. One egg. Salt and pepper. Crushed cornflakes.

Mash potatoes; add parsley, beaten egg, fish, salt and pepper. Shape into flat cakes, toss in cornflakes and fry gently in shallow fat, turning to cook both sides.

Mint and Egg Pie: Line a sandwich-tin with pastry, and break in three whole eggs. Sprinkle over these chopped mint, small pieces of butter, and salt and pepper. Cover with a pastry lid, and cook in a fairly hot oven, 420°F., until golden-brown.

Chive and Cream Cheese Potatoes: Bake some large potatoes in the oven about an hour until soft. Cut them in half and put the insides into a bowl. Chop some chive (cut it with scissors) and mash it into the potato, with 1 oz. cream cheese for each potato; add salt and pepper. Pile it back into the potato shells, and put them into the oven to heat through.

Sage and Onion Stuffing: 4 oz. breadcrumbs, 6 sage leaves, 2 onions, 2 ozs. suet, salt and pepper, a small egg. Boil the onions (chopped) until soft. Drain off water, and mix with the other ingredients. Form into small cakes, and fry gently until well cooked. Serve with sausages.

Bay Leaves can be added to meat stews (one will be sufficient), but my favourite way is to float one on top of a rice-pudding while it is slowly cooking. Try it—it gives the pudding a delicious flavour.

Gillian on Safari

by David Harwood

Photographs by J. H. Mortimer

Gillian Ramsey, of the 2nd Bradford-on-Avon (Christ Church) Guide Company, did not travel more than thirty miles and did not have to cross the boundaries of her native county of Wiltshire to go on an African-style safari. She went to Longleat, the stately home and estate of the Marquess of Bath, near Warminster. She was going to take a special look at the wildlife there.

First of all, Gillian met Roger Cawley, Manager of the Lions of Longleat, who gave her a special pass and sent a radio message to Rodney Brown, one of the many "white hunters", game wardens and other staff. It was arranged that we should meet him in the East African

Game Park, an open area of some hundred acres of grassland.

In this park such birds and animals as ostriches, zebra, Ankole cattle and the largest herd of giraffe outside Africa are free to roam as they please. Visitors, too, can get out of their cars and watch the animals, though, as the game wardens remind people over loud-hailers, the animals are not pets and it is advisable to keep a reasonable distance away from them. With their enormous horns the pair of Ankole cattle, known as Nina and Frederick, look rather frightening, but they are the quietest and safest of the animals in the Park. In Africa they are as common as farm cattle are in this country. You just have to be careful when they shake their heads to rid themselves of flies.

Most of the vehicles patrolling the wildlife areas carry special equipment, and Mr. Brown's Land Rover was no exception. In one of the photographs Gillian is talking over the radio by which the

Gillian talks by radio telephone from the safari car

35

In Pets' Corner Gillian chats to Fairy Corrella, a miniature Shetland pony only 28 inches high. A four-month-old donkey decides to join in the conversation

"white hunter" communicates directly to the other vehicles or to the central control. With the other microphone, the driver can use the Tannoy (a loud-speaker attached to the front of the vehicle) to warn visitors of any danger or to remind those in the other reserves to keep their windows shut. For emergencies like break-downs and accidents, a set of switches will set off various noises—a "yelp", a "wail", or a siren. Clipped into the roof of the cab is a special double-barrelled gun which fires either blanks or solid-ball shot. Gillian realised that she would be well protected when she went into the reserves!

Gillian climbed into the Land Rover with Mr. Brown and stopped in the Monkey Jungle, which is inhabited by two hundred baboons. These animals have hot tempers and can bite, so feeding them is not normally allowed. Under Mr Brown's watchful eye, however, Gillian was permitted to hand one baboon—at arm's length—a piece of bread. As well as bread, the baboons eat fruit, vege-tables, maize and vitamin cubes that look like grass and leaves.

For the next hour or so Gillian stayed in the Land Rover. With the sweltering summer sun beating down, she had a grandstand view of the majestic lions lazing on grassy mounds and under the trees. In the cheetah reserve, too, she saw the animals stretched out in the shade under the trees.

When the last of the large gates clanged behind her and she was out in the park, near Longleat House, Gillian was hot and hungry and more than ready for a long, cold drink and a bite of lunch.

The next place she explored was Pets' Corner. Here she met Jenny Ayscough, who looks after a large number of different types of animals and birds, which children can see at close quarters. There were lion-cubs, macaws, pigs, guinea-pigs, llamas, goats, and many more. Again Gillian was given VIP treatment and allowed into an enclosure to have a really close look at the rabbits inside and outside their beautifully built house. She was also able to take the halter of Fairy Corrella, a miniature Shetland pony, who

was four years old and fully grown, yet only twenty-eight inches high. The donkey you can see in the photograph came over to make friends with her. He was just four *months* old and still growing!

After Pets' Corner, Gillian went back to the lion and cheetah reserves to watch the animals being fed. It was then that she realised just how dangerous these animals can be, and the reason for all the warning notices and the safety precautions. Instead of lying about like large domestic cats, they were prowling about, growling, roaring and baring their teeth. The lions clawed at the meat-cage on the back of the truck as whole cows' heads were thrown out to them. The cheetahs, reckoned to be the fastest of land animals, pounced on to and around the Land Rover, eager to get their teeth into a chicken.

Gillian's special safari was almost over, but she was in for an extra special sur-

Gillian watches the cheetahs being fed—from a safe distance

Gillian makes friends with Leo, a lion-cub

side their home, giving Leo, a four-week-old lion-cub who had been abandoned by his mother, his afternoon bottle of milk. Mary Chipperfield is a daughter in the famous Chipperfield family, who have for three hundred years worked with wild animals. She very kindly let Gillian watch the feeding of Leo and of a six-week-old tiger-cub called Suki. Then, much to her delight, Gillian was allowed to fondle and play with Leo and Suki on the lawn for about half an hour. How would *you* like to handle a real live lion? This one, Leo, was worth no less than three hundred pounds.

The eight hours at Longleat had sped by. It was time to be making tracks for home. Gillian had discovered a lot of things which were very useful to her as a Guide.

Back at home, she did a report for the Company's log book and wrote an article for Wiltshire's Scout magazine, *The White Horse Express*. She had met a number of interesting people and she had learnt new facts about many animals and birds. She came away from Longleat with a lot of ideas for making a start on badges, including Stalker, Naturalist and Observer.

prise. When she went to say thank you to Mr. Cawley, she found his wife, Mary Chipperfield, sitting on the terrace out-

---

HOW TO MAKE "GHOST FLOWERS"

by Andrew J. Smith

SULPHUR BURNING IN SAUCER

STICKY TAPE HOLDING STEMS TO TOP OF JAR

To make "ghost flowers" you will need a jamjar with a tight-fitting top, some sulphur from a chemist, and some brightly coloured flowers.

First put about half a teaspoon of sulphur in a small saucer and light it; then quickly place it in a jamjar and put the lid on securely.

Next select three or four blooms and tie the stalks together. Then take the lid off the jamjar and attach the stalks to the inside of the lid with a piece of sticky tape and quickly replace the lid.

The powerful bleaching agent of the sulphur will in time bleach the flowers to a "ghostly" white. You will also be able to preserve them by pressing them between sheets of blotting-paper.

MOSS

It has instructions to enhance
A brook or any nook where fairies dance,
To smooth the sharpest edges of a stone,
To carpet shade that grass has never known.
Of course you know moss does not grow.
It is woven on the magic loom of spring—
A green unmatched by any planted thing—
So summer in her flowered print may wear
A touch of royal velvet here and there.

by *SUMNER BARLOW*

Reprinted by permission from the *Christian Science Monitor*

39

THERE'S

When you're hiking through the woods in your enjoyment of the out-of-doors, you probably pay no attention to old, hollow trees.

If you did spot a hollow tree, you might see the bleached, silver-grey wood stripped and peeled by the wind, rain and snow. And you might think the tree has lost its beauty and usefulness.

But look closely at the base of the trunk. See the fresh wood chips? They are a very good sign that this dead tree still provides a home for some lively forest creatures.

A hole at the base of the great trunk may be the entrance to a badger's sett. Perhaps he and his sow are at this moment fast asleep underground among the deep roots. Another hole round the back could be a rabbit's back exit.

Look closely at the side of the trunk and up about ten feet or so and you might see a burned and charred, oddly shaped hole. This is pretty good evidence a bee-hunter tried to smoke out a swarm of bees to collect their honey.

Walk closer to the grey trunk shell and examine the countless tiny round holes busy insects have made. You may even see long, even scratches on the trunk made by the badgers' claws.

Want to see how alive this hollow tree really is? Well, move nothing but your

LIFE IN THAT DEAD TREE

eyes. Animals can sense the least bit of unusual movement in the woods.

After ten or fifteen minutes of silent, motionless study don't be surprised to detect movement from a lofty perch or knot-hole. A squirrel has decided to come out and sun himself; or out from one of the many trunk holes a woodpecker may poke its crimson head.

Woodpeckers use their sharp-pointed beaks to drill and chisel through the outer trunk to capture insects and make a nest. Their, *rap, rap* hammerings echo through the forest and can hardly be mistaken.

Maybe, nearer dark, you'll even hear an owl hoot from the darkness of one of the holes in the upper trunk to show that he's guarding his hollow-tree home.

As long shadows fall and streak across the forest floor, be ready for more movement. Depending on how much patience you have to watch, you might just see a colony of bats slip noiselessly out from an upper branch for a night's flight and feeding. They return before sunrise to sleep in the hollow trunk, where they hang upside down by their feet on the inside walls.

When you're ready to leave, mark your hollow tree for another secret visit. You may want to return soon.

Reprinted by permission from the *Christian Science Monitor*

THE CRAFTY KINGFISHERS

by RIKKI TAYLOR

When the Kingfishers set out for Patrol camp they were travelling light.

"Where is your kit?" asked their Guider.

The P.L. laughed. "When we reach the field I can turn the GATE in four moves into my PACK. — **G A T E** / **P A C K**

"The campsite is by a lake," remarked the Kingfisher Second.

The Kingfishers cheered. "In that case we can make a TENT in three moves into a BOAT." — **T E N T** / **B O A T**

"I've lost my dish," wailed Jenny, the youngest of the Kingfishers. — **M I S T**

"Not to worry," smiled the P.L., who took the MIST and in three moves turned it into a DISH. — **D I S H**

The Second found it hard work using a SAW. — **S A W**

The P.L. grinned. "In three moves we can have all the wood CUT." — **C U T** / **W O O D**

The Kingfishers in four moves turned WOOD into a FIRE. — **F I R E**

Jenny opened a TIN and in two moves made TEA. — **T I N** / **T E A**

But she boiled the dixie on a STOVE, which in two moves she had made from a STILE. — **S T O V E** / **S T I L E**

In only three moves the CAMP looked just like HOME. — **C A M P** / **H O M E**

From across the meadows came the sound of the church BELL, which in three moves turned into a PEAL. — **B E L L** / **P E A L**

By altering one letter only at each move, can you do the same as the Kingfishers?

WHICH PATROL BIRD?

by S. King

If you write the correct answers in the squares, the letters in circles will spell the name of a Guide Patrol bird.

1. Britain's best-loved wild bird
2. Rare bird mostly found in Scottish Highlands
3. The haunt of the otter
4. Tiny animal that never stops eating
5. Water-bird that often stands still for a long time.

ANSWERS

1—Robin; 2—Eagle; 3—River; 4—Shrew; 5—Heron
PATROL BIRD: Raven

"BE PREPARED"

In Hyderabad You Had To Be
Says E. Phillips

When I was a Guider in Hyderabad about forty years ago we were never in danger of forgetting the Guide motto, "Be Prepared", for when you come to adapt Western ways to Eastern customs there are plenty of surprises.

Brownies are called Bluebirds in Hyderabad, and the first puzzle was how to determine, especially in the rural Packs, when they should fly up to Guides, since most were quite vague about their age. In the end we borrowed the horse-coper's method and looked at their teeth: when they had lost all their milk teeth they were ready to be Guides!

Uniform was the next problem. Companies were usually attached to a school, and, though there were exceptions, the majority in each Company would be Muslim or Hindu or Christian. Mission-school Companies, or Anglo-Indian girls in other groups, often wore "English" uniforms, but more commonly local clothes were adopted. Our Muslim girls wore white pyjama trousers and the kurta, or muslim shirt, with a blue dupatta—six yards of rolled muslin worn over the shoulder and tucked into the top of the pyjama—while the Hindu Guides wore long, full, navy skirts and white tucked-in blouses with a plain blue sari. Parsis sometimes wore the English overall, but

the older ones always wore a sari with a border—the uniform one had gold trefoils on the blue. Parsis were generally among the most Westernised communities, but one could find their customs disconcerting too. We were once in camp where senior Guides and Guiders took it in turn to see that the fires were lighted for the breakfast cookery. There was also a bath rota. On one occasion our most reliable Parsi leader failed to light up, and it was only after very tactful questioning that we found out that, since to her fire was sacred, she could not touch it before she had been "purified" by her bath—and she was on the mid-morning rota for that!

Our Muslim Company had a single Hindu member, and on a picnic she could only eat a banana—and that with her back turned to the rest of us—though she took part with enthusiasm in activities which did not involve food.

Our Christmas party, given by the Commissioner, was a joint festivity in which six or seven Companies, representing a whole gamut of religious beliefs, joined. Many of the Hindu girls came from very poor districts—some of them

from low-caste groups. Fruit always made up a large part of the menu because so many other kinds of food might unwittingly offend against the religious rules of one or other of the communities to which the girls belonged. But it was very important for the organisers to understand the "dastur" which governed party behaviour. "Dastur" might be translated as "custom" or "convention". It means that way of doing something which is traditionally acceptable. Unlike the behaviour implied by the old Scottish manners rule, "eat your fill but pocket none", it was "dastur" in Hyderabad that the tucked-into-skirts blouses would be used as pockets to hold the extra oranges and bananas and pomegranates—and the Commissioner always made sure that there were plenty of extras. It was very important that the fruit should not be offered until after the games of "dodge ball" and

the relay races, for no one would want to risk running about after the fruit was served and so dropping the extra food!

But it would be very wrong to see Guiding as something so alien that it must change out of recognition in its Indian surroundings. True, some details had to adapt. Girls in close purdah (a word meaning "curtain", but used to mean the keeping of girls and women in strict seclusion in a women's section of their homes and forbidding them to go outside unless heavily veiled and closely escorted) could not be expected to be able to direct a stranger to the post-office or police-station, and, for many not in purdah, this was still an unrealistic demand since the occasion could not arise in their remote villages. But the principle of helping others at all times was of special importance in a society where the acceptance of "Allah's will" often has a stultifying effect on all kinds of aid. Until the late Canon Tyndale Biscoe taught his schoolboys in Kashmir to swim and life-save, countless lives were lost by drowning because no one attempted to save those who fell in river or lake. Even minor accidents were ignored rather than dealt with.

In Britain, we tended to look upon the proficiency tests as encouraging competence in first aid or cookery, in knitting or laundry work, but in Hyderabad their importance lay in breaking down the barriers against having anything to do with "menial" activities. In a country where many kinds of work were regarded with disgust the importance of earning Guide badges lay in the fact that girls of all classes and creeds, whether their fathers were great landowners or illiterate, unskilled labourers, had each to do exactly the same things. It took quite a long time to persuade many girls from wealthy

families that a cake made by a servant did not qualify them for a Cook badge!

Thirty years ago a school certificate would be accepted by many Hyderabad grooms in lieu of a dowry. Its possession was, therefore, a step to matrimony, the sole respectable career. Our pupils openly sympathised with our failure, for which they held our parents culpably at fault, to have gained husbands before we reached our middle twenties! But the practice in elementary leadership which these girls had as Guides did more than school certificates when, during the war and the independence which followed, they came out from purdah to become nurses and secretaries and teachers and the wives of diplomats moving in international society. Some of them must have remembered the Commissioner's Christmas parties and their "badge" work on Saturday afternoons in the school compound.

WHAT'S THE MESSAGE?

The 1st Rickshires are camping in a large meadow this year. What message is Q.M. sending to the Cook Patrol?   —J.M.H.

COOK PATROL
"I have to cook everything on an open fire since Joan came back from camp"

JUMBLE LUCK

by LIZABETH SLEEP

Jane shivered in the cold wind. "Let's not bother," she said as they reached the last cottage in the lane. "Our bag is almost full and you know how poor Miss Minton is. I'm sure that she won't have anything to give us."

"We ought to try, just the same," Kathleen insisted. "We've asked for jumble at every other house in the road. Miss Minton would be very hurt if she found out and thought that we hadn't bothered to ask her."

She opened the garden gate, led the way up the garden path and knocked on the door of the tiny cottage.

"Good afternoon, Miss Minton!" Kathleen said politely, as a little grey-haired lady answered the door. "We're collecting for our jumble sale."

"Come in, my dears," Miss Minton invited. "Come in out of the cold."

She shepherded them inside. The room, with its tiny fire, was not much warmer than the lane outside, the Guides decided.

Miss Minton gave a shiver as she pulled her old cardigan closer round her shoulders, but she smiled at the two girls.

"I'd like to help you. We didn't have Guides when I was a girl, so I never had the chance to be one, though I'm sure I should have enjoyed it. But I don't know what I can give you for your sale." She stared thoughtfully round her rather bare room. "You'd better sit down, my dears." She pointed to a battered sofa in one corner. "I'll go upstairs and see if I can find something for you up there."

The two Guides sat cautiously down on the creaking sofa as Miss Minton went up the narrow stairs. They could hear her pulling open drawers and closing cupboard doors.

"I do wish she would hurry up," Jane muttered impatiently.

Miss Minton came back at last with a small white tablecloth in her hand. "I used to have some more of these, but this is the only one that I can find now. I'm afraid it's rather old, but the lace is very pretty. Will it be all right for your sale?" she asked anxiously.

"It will be lovely," Kathleen smiled. "I'm sure lots of people will want to buy it." She folded the cloth up and put it on top of their already bulging bag. "Thank you very much, Miss Minton."

Miss Minton waved happily from her window as

"We're collecting for our jumble sale"

Kathleen tucked the cloth out of sight as Miss Minton approached

they set off down the lane. As soon as her cottage was out of sight Jane wrinkled her nose.

"Fancy giving us an old thing like that to sell!" she said. "It's not even clean!"

"Of course it is!" Kathleen was indignant. "It looks a bit yellow because it is so old."

"Well, I bet no one buys it," Jane said.

At two o'clock on the following Saturday the jumble sale began. The goods for sale were arranged on long wooden tables all round the sides of the village hall. Behind each stall were two Guides, ready to sell. The doors to the hall were thrown open and a crowd of would-be customers poured inside and clustered round the stalls. Kathleen and Jane were soon hard at work.

After two hours there was very little left to sell on their stall, and they had time to look round and see what was happening on the other stalls.

"There's Miss Minton!" said Jane. "She's bought that nice blanket your mother knitted."

"Oh, I am glad!" Kathleen said. "It's pretty and it will keep her warm." She looked down at the few things on the stall that were still unsold. "I hope Miss Minton doesn't come over here. No one has bought that cloth she gave us. She'll be very upset if she sees it still here."

"She's coming this way now," Jane said.

"Then I'll buy the cloth myself." Kathleen made up her mind quickly. She paid for it and tucked it out of sight behind the stall just as Miss Minton came across.

"My!" Miss Minton said. "You haven't many things left to sell, have you?"

"Very few," said Kathleen.

Miss Minton leaned over the stall. "I do hope somebody liked my tablecloth enough to buy it?" she said shyly.

Kathleen nodded. "Somebody did," she replied. "It was bought only a few minutes ago."

The old lady's cheeks turned pink with pleasure, and Kathleen's last regrets for her spent pocket-money vanished.

At last almost everything had been sold. The last customer left, and the Guider began to count up the money. "We've done very well," she announced at last. "We've taken over twelve pounds. Well done, everyone!"

It was almost dark when Kathleen arrived home. She hurried upstairs and spread the little cloth out on her bed so that she could see it properly. In two days' time it would be her mother's birthday, and Kathleen had been keeping her pocket-money to buy some flowers. She counted the rest of her savings and sighed. Now that she had bought the cloth there was only about enough money left for a birthday card. Could she give the cloth as a birthday gift? She bit her lip and frowned. Would her mother mind about the cloth being old and yellow? She decided to risk it.

Her mother had lots of cards on the morning of her birthday, and Kathleen thought her present looked very small beside the larger ones of her elder brothers and sisters. Her mother opened one parcel after another. Daddy had bought perfume. There was a big box of chocolates from Kathleen's eldest sister, who had just started work, and her little brother brought out a plant that he had grown all by himself.

At last she came to Kathleen's present. Kathleen held her breath as her mother undid the paper, lifted out the cloth, and held it up. Then she put it down and stared at Kathleen.

"Where on earth did you get this?" she demanded.

"Don't you like it?" Kathleen was almost in tears.

"Like it?" her mother said. "It's absolutely lovely, but it is valuable."

Kathleen gazed at her incredulously. "Valuable?"

"It's the lace," her mother explained. "This is real hand-made antique lace and very beautiful. It must be worth quite a bit of money. Where did you get it?"

Kathleen explained.

"I'm afraid you'll have to take it back," her mother said gently. "Miss Minton obviously doesn't know its value. After breakfast we must go round and tell her."

Miss Minton could hardly believe her ears. She stared from Kathleen to her mother in amazement.

"I don't understand," she said at last. "I thought it was just a lace cloth. It belonged to my mother. I've got several, but I've never used them. You need pretty china to put on pretty cloths, and I've never had enough money for that."

"If you have more of that lace," Kathleen's mother said, "you'll be able to buy pretty china if you want it."

"I have more upstairs." Miss Minton scurried off and came back presently with a pile of lace-work. "I can hardly believe it," she said happily. "If you are sure it's worth money, I shall be able to have some things to make the cottage more comfortable."

"I'm quite sure of its value," Kathleen's mother assured her. She added her cloth to the pile. "I can't possibly keep this, of course."

"But you must!" Miss Minton insisted. "I'd like you to have it."

"I'd love to have it," Kathleen's mother said. "It's the nicest birthday present I've ever had."

"That's settled, then." Miss Minton beamed, and her eyes twinkled as she looked at Kathleen. "Don't forget to come to me next time you have a jumble sale. I might find some more valuable things in the cottage if I search round!"

—DODSWORTH.—

"What time's breakfast in bed?"

PLASTIC POTTERY

Here's a quick and effective way of making a plastic flower-pot or fancy container. All you need is an empty yogurt carton of plastic and a saucepan of nearly boiling water.

Put the empty yogurt pot on a flat surface. Leave the boiled water for a few seconds to cool, then pour it carefully into the yogurt pot—fairly quickly, so that you will have enough time to "mould" the plastic pot into your desired shape. Remember, though, that you can only shape your pot by pulling it up or down while the water remains at a temperature that will keep the plastic pliable.

With this method you can make a variety of attractive containers. It's a good idea to paint your finished "pottery" and perhaps give it a coat of varnish to produce a "glazed" appearance.—**A.T.S.**

DO GUIDES LACK A SENSE OF HUMOUR?

ASKS THE EDITOR

Many Guides write in to the *Girl Guide Annual*. Mostly, they write to say that they have enjoyed a particular contribution or to point out a mistake. Sometimes they write appreciatively to say how much they enjoyed the annual; sometimes they report that they knitted the doll on page so-and-so for the Toymaker badge and it was most successful; and sometimes they ask for more information about a subject.

All the letters are welcome, but what makes me ask the question posed in the title above is that no Guide has ever written to indicate that she screamed with laughter at the cartoons or held her side in stitches of mirth at the comic verses on page 22 (or 99).

Now, it may be that the cartoons weren't funny enough to raise an outright laugh or the comic verses comical enough to tickle the ribs; or is it that Guides as a whole lack a sense of humour?

Most people laugh at slapstick, so if there was a cartoon of a Guider shooting up through the roof of her tent while a Guide looking on confides to her friend that she put a thistle in the Guider's sleeping-bag would you laugh? The *Girl Guide Annual* tends to favour a less crude type of humour and presents cartoons of the kind that shows the new Guide com-

plaining bitterly to the Guider-in-charge at camp that there's no place for her to plug in her television set.

One of the funny things about humour is that it isn't always funny—or, rather, it isn't funny to all people. Personally, I love the slightly subtle type of humour, as expressed, for instance, in the saying that a girl invented high heels because she was tired of being kissed on the forehead. Yes, I like that—do you?

Well, I'll go on printing cartoons and comic verse in the *Girl Guide Annual*, hoping desperately that you'll enjoy 'em. I can't believe that you do lack a sense of humour, because I've heard of Guides suffering appalling climatic conditions at camp and then going home and declaring that "we had a smashng time" and "we're looking forward to going again next year". That shows a delightful, wry sense of humour—or does it? It can't be, can it, that they *weren't* joking?

Well, I love to laugh. I only hope you do too, because every now and again in the *Girl Guide Annual* you'll find a determined attempt to make you!

DOES THIS MAKE YOU LAUGH?

"It looks very nice, but has it only got one room?"

49

Letter To Jane

by K. M. Cowley

Dear Jane,

I do hope you are enjoying your first experience of camping. The weather is good to you, so far! I expect camping nowadays is much less rigorous than it was when I was in Guides, forty years or so ago.

Do you have refinements to make life easier—lilos or camp-beds, gas burners for your cooking, Elsan toilets? They would give you more freedom, I think, to enjoy your camping.

My first camp was a mixture of fears and delights! I was terrified of beetles, and went armed with a tin of Keating's Bug Powder (I wonder if it is still sold) to sprinkle round the straw-filled sack that was my bed. We had to go to the nearby farm for our supply of straw. All the softest had gone when I got there, and it made an uncomfortable, prickly bed, believe me!

We were kept awake most of the first night by a fellow tent-mate who filled her hair with metal curlers (no rollers then) before settling down for the night. She believed in being glamorous with a head full of tight little sausage curls! Curls were very much sought after in those days. She was an hour putting them

in, and rattled them about the tin as she sorted out the sizes; it sounded like a scrap-merchant's wagon rattling along the road.

We settled down with a sigh of relief when they were all in, and then up she sprang, shouting that she was being invaded by earwigs! By this time it was quite dark, and as no one had a torch we took her word for it that the little dark things we could faintly see were indeed earwigs. Out came the mallets. We all started bashing away with them, bashing a few toes as well. It wasn't until dawn that we found that the "earwigs" were bits of grass and leaves!

Our washing arrangements were very primitive. Perhaps they still are. We had little cubicles made with hessian and an enamelled bowl balanced on a stand made out of three (or was it four?) twiggy

From Forty Years Ago

branches lashed together. Sometimes the branches stood up to the weight of the bowl of water (cold) and sometimes they collapsed under the strain. It depended on who had done the lashing! When the sun shone, the hessian was transparent, so it didn't do to go for a wash when the sun was shining!

Our loos—or latrines, to give them their proper name—were even more primitive. There was a six-feet-deep, two-feet-wide trench, with rough boxes across at decent intervals. The boxes had holes cut in them, and one sat over the hole! A little shovel was kept near by and one shovelled enough soil in off the bank to cover one's tracks! Needless to say, the soil didn't always go in the right place! There was a hessian screen round that was transparent like the washing cubicles when the sun shone! The flies, as

you can imagine, had a good time, in spite of bunches of elder hung on the hessian. Flies were supposed to dislike elder, but our camping flies weren't worried about it!

We were all constipated, because we put off the moment of going as long as we possibly could, and the middle of the week found us queueing up at Captain's tent with a mug of water, into which she ladled a good helping of salts! The loos were even worse to visit after that—particularly for your Aunty Joyce, who had to run with her precious letter from home, unopened, in her hand. The worst happened—she dropped it in the trench! She either had to leave it there unread, which was unthinkable, or climb down for it. So she climbed down for it!

I wonder what your meals are like nowadays. I remember how absolutely wonderful thick slices of bread, spread with marge and jam, tasted eaten outside, with the smoke from the wood cooking-fire adding to the flavour. There never seemed to be quite enough bacon to go round, I remember. Aunty Joyce and I always seemed to be at the end of the line, so we got the burnt bits, or none at all.

We also got landed with the awful job of cleaning the billycans at the end of the week. They were all sooted up with the wood smoke, and we had a terrible job getting them clean, because hot water was always scarce. I don't know about Guide camps now, but I hear that school camps are very sophisticated, with big boilers always full of hot water, and marquees for dining-rooms with tables and chairs, and cooking done on portable gas cookers! Not such fun, though!

The highlight of each day was the sing-song round the camp-fire in the evening. It was most satisfying to sit round on groundsheets, cross-legged, with the flames leaping up into the dusk and all the scents of the evening filling the air. Fortunately, the loos were too far away to compete!

The old songs never seemed to grow stale, no matter how often we bellowed them out. I wonder if they still have the same appeal for you, who have been brought up on "pop". There was a feeling of "belonging" at those camp-fires. All over the world, probably, camp-fires were burning, with Guides of all colours and creeds sitting round them, singing their heads off.

A big mug of cocoa finished off the day, and we were ready to bed down on our straw palliasses and wait for the "metal curler rattler" to do her nightly stint before we could get to sleep.

We had to have one hour's rest after the midday meal, when we could write letters or read or just snooze. I wonder if you still have it? If you do, please write and tell me all about modern camping and how it compares with ours of forty years ago.

Forty years ago! Yes, it's a long time since I camped with the Guides, but I shall never forget it. Happy, unforgettable days!

With love,
Aunty Kath

WHICH PATROL FOR EMMA?

Emma is going up to Guides from the Brownie Pack. Draw the shapes in the frames below into the blank frames with the same numbers and you will complete Emma's Patrol emblem.

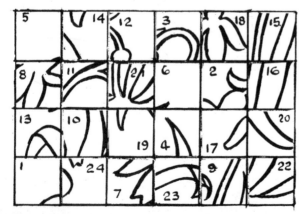
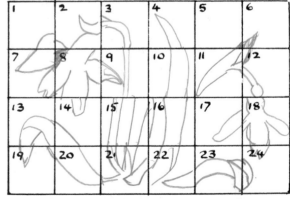

SNOWDROPS

Feather Finding's Fun

Says S. A. Clarke

Fine feathers make fine birds—or so the old saying goes. Well, fine feathers that birds have lost can help you to enjoy the out-of-doors and to gain the Collector badge. They can also link up with the Bird-Watcher and Naturalist badges.

Birds lose their feathers from several causes—when they moult, when they have a set-to with an enemy, or when they unexpectedly fly through a thicket. Late summer and early autumn are the usual moulting times for most wild birds; but you can still find feathers at any time of the year in places like shallow pools, where the birds go for a cooler, or at dusting places along the roadside—and this includes city streets as well as country lanes—where the birds thrash about in their comforting dust baths.

If you accidentally flush (and that means frighten) a bird whilst walking near a thicket, you will quite often find a feather or two that have fluttered to the ground. As a Guide, of course, you won't scare a bird purposely to obtain a feather.

Feeding and nesting spots are other places where you are almost certain to be able to pick up a feather or two. You'll be careful, won't you, not to disturb the nest in any way?

A good thing about collecting the cast-off "clothes" of birds is that you don't have to set off with that object in mind. When you picnic, camp, or simply take a stroll in a wood or field or across a common, feathers of every size, shape, form and colour are likely to lie in places where they will catch your eye. Even while going shopping, you may still be able to pick up the quill of a city pigeon or some humble brown-grey wisps from a sparrow. However large or small they may be, they are quite marvellous things to study.

How to Begin

To begin your feather collecting, you should borrow or buy a guide-book; this will help you to identify your feathers. There's sure to be one in your local public library. Don't be afraid to ask for it if you can't find it easily on the shelves yourself. If you happen to have a natural history museum (or such a section in your local museum) near you, then

53

you are really in luck's way, for you will be able to compare your finds with the bird collections there.

Ordinary paper envelopes will do to store your feathers in for a start, but later, as your collection and your knowledge grow, you may find plastic "display"

stemmed as are the flight feathers, about which I shall tell you in a moment. They are designed for the protection of the bird from hot sun and other weather conditions, and are often the first covering the baby bird has for quite a while.

Contour feathers are the second group.

envelopes more suitable. You can mount the feathers on stiff paper, or keep them in a special tray or box. The test for the Collector badge requires your collection to be well arranged, labelled and identified.

What is a feather? It is what is known as an epidermal growth, not like the hair of a mammal, but more nearly like the scale of a reptile. Though there are, of course, all kinds of varieties, there are three main types, and these should be made the basis of your collection.

Three Kinds of Feathers

Down feathers are the first kind. They are soft and small, and not strong-

These form the main body covering of the growing bird. Though they are quite firm and develop strongly they are often downy at the base.

Flight feathers are the most fascinating of all. Even a jet plane's structure cannot compare with a bird's wonderfully constructed flight feathers, and that's an astounding thought, isn't it?

The flight feathers are the large strong-stemmed feathers of wings and tail. In a flight feather there is a strong, tapering central shaft or stem. The thicker lower end is called the "quill". This is hollow. The upper part, which is filled with a firm pith (or marrow), is called the "rachis". You will soon find that the whole shaft (or stem) will stand a great deal of bending before breaking—and when you see birds battling against winds and bad weather you easily understand why.

Branching outwards on each side of the shaft are hundreds of thin structures called "barbs", which form the feather's body or vane.

Along each side of each "barb" are tiny hair-like branches, which are called "barbules". Those on the side towards the outer tip of the feather are hooked; these are called "hamuli". Those on the side nearest the base of the feather are curved and notched at the end; they are the "ciliae".

When a feather is in perfect condition, each "barb" is hooked to its adjoining "barb", and it is this wonderful design of interlocking notches and hooks which enables the feather to hold air. If this were not so, the bird would be unable to fly, because pressure on the feather in attempted flight would cause the "barbs" to separate and the air to slip through.

A magnifying glass or microscope will enable you to study all those wonderful details which go to make that marvellous structure—a bird's flight feather.

Arranging Your Feathers

How to arrange your collection will be your next thought, and here are several suggestions. The simplest way is to make a collection according to colour, or according to the markings of the feathers. Another way is to keep a sheet of stiff paper for each species, and on this sheet mount and label a down feather, a contour feather, and a flight feather (from wing or tail).

Yet another interesting method is to mount several feathers of one type on one sheet—such as a flight feather from each of ten different types of birds—and several of another type on another sheet, and so on.

Whichever way you choose, you can be sure you will make a most interesting and unusual collection, one that it will give you pride to build up and show.

Partridge

Swallow

Blackbird

Yellowhammer

Woodpecker

Pheasant

THE STRANGE AFFAIR AT FOUR OAKS

by KENNETH MOORE

Angela was quite taken aback at her mother's remark. "Not go to the sea? We've always gone, and now I can swim it'll be more fun than ever."

She listened gloomily to her mother's explanation that, since her father was going on a business trip to America, they had taken a cottage for the holidays. Even a whole eight weeks in the country didn't seem sufficient compensation for missing the sea.

On the last lap of their railway journey to the West Country, Angela and her mother shared a compartment with two ladies. Apparently these ladies had been house-hunting and had had unfortunate experiences. One of them, it seemed, concerned a cottage called Four Oaks. One lady said: "We very nearly got taken in over that cottage."

"Yes, indeed," said the other. "It makes me shudder to think what a narrow escape we had."

The man pushed rudely past them and shouted at the clerk

This was a scrap of overheard conversation which Angela normally would have soon forgotten. As it was, the happenings of the next few days were to bring the remarks back to her more than once.

As they were talking to the clerk in the estate agent's office and collecting the key to their cottage, a man burst in. He pushed rudely past them and said angrily to the clerk: "Look here, I telephoned early this morning and told you to remove that card about my cottage from your window. It's still there. I wish to goodness you'd do what you're asked straight away."

The clerk did her best to calm him down, and taking the card from the window said: "Have you sold the property, then, Mr. Benson?"

"That's as may be," he retorted rudely, "but I don't want people snooping round Four Oaks while I'm away."

While the clerk was apologising for the interruption, Angela caught sight of something through the window, and said: "Won't be a minute! I must have a word with someone across the street."

In fact, her mother had to wait outside the office several minutes before Angela returned. When she did so, Angela said excitedly: "That's a terrific piece of luck! That girl I spied in Guide uniform belongs to the local Company. Her name's Margaret and she's Second of the Kingfishers. I told her I wanted to work for the Naturalist badge while I'm here, and she's sure their Guider will let me join in some of their outings."

Soon they were in a taxi on their way to Jessamine Cottage. As they turned a corner, they were surprised to see again the man, Benson, who had been in the estate agent's office. He was covering up a FOR SALE notice. This, then, must be Four Oaks. He looked up and scowled sourly.

"What an unpleasant man!" exclaimed Angela.

The next turn of the lane brought them to Jessamine Cottage. When Angela looked round the cottage her spirits rose. It certainly was a pretty place, and since meeting the Guide in the village she felt distinctly happier. It would be fun meeting other Guides. Then she thought of the talk between the ladies in the train and the odd behaviour of the owner of Four Oaks. There certainly seemed to be something strange about Four Oaks and its owner.

Next morning, while they were still engaged in

"He's there!" Sally whispered

the business of settling in, Margaret, the Guide Angela had already met, called round. She brought an invitation for Angela to join the Kingfishers on an outing to the swimming-baths. Angela was glad to accept. When she went on to ask about the local wild life, Margaret said: "You should talk to Sally about that. She's a bit boisterous, but she's dead keen on Nature and birds. You'll meet her tomorrow."

They were still talking when there was a knock at the door. Angela answered it and found a lady asking for Four Oaks. The lady was glad to learn that it was quite near. About a quarter of an hour later, Angela heard raised voices.

"Oh, dear!" she murmured. "I hope it's not that horrid man being nasty to the lady. Perhaps we'd better go and see if she's all right." She explained to Margaret what had happened the previous day.

The two Guides went off down the lane. As they turned the corner, they saw and heard Benson shouting. He had clearly lost his temper and was kicking viciously at one wheel of a car. In the car was the lady who had called at Jessamine Cottage. She seemed too flustered to get the car started.

"I say, there!" Margaret called out. "What goes on? Can we help?"

Benson, taken by surprise, stopped kicking the wheel. The diversion helped the lady. She put the car into gear and moved off.

Benson scowled at the girls and hurried back into the house.

As they walked back to Jessamine Cottage Margaret said: "That man, Benson, is really a foreigner in these parts. It's quite odd really. He bought Four Oaks a month or so ago, and now he's trying to sell it."

"Then why is he so rude to people? Look how he frightened that lady."

"It does seem strange, doesn't it?"

Later that day Angela met the rest of the Kingfishers. First she was introduced to Judy, the Patrol Leader, a tall girl with chestnut hair, and to Liz, a studious-looking girl who wore glasses. Last to join them were Sally, who had a mop of unruly fair hair and chattered gaily non-stop, and Rosemary, who was quiet and neat and had dark hair.

Angela was glad she could swim, though most of the girls were streets ahead of her. Sally, in particular, swam and dived with the skill of a mermaid. Of all the girls only Rosemary was in the novice class as a swimmer. When the two had a race, Angela was just able to win.

It was all thoroughly enjoyable, and only when they were waiting for the bus back was there any awkward moment. Judy counted the girls as they got in the bus and found that Sally was missing. Indeed, she would have been left behind had not Judy persuaded the driver to wait another minute. As it was, he was just about to start off when Sally appeared, running. She was quite unabashed by the scoldings she received.

"My goldfish have finished all their ants' eggs. I just had to get more. I can't let them starve, can I?"

On the way back, Angela arranged with Sally to go on a Nature expedition. Margaret turned round from the seat in front and said: "You'll need to go well prepared if you go with Sally. She's never content unless she's scrambling through hedges or jumping over brooks."

Two days later Angela set out with Sally. She was wearing jeans. When they drew near a barn, Sally cautioned: "We must go quietly now. Owls have good hearing, and unusual noises disturb them."

Angela was quite surprised at her companion's seriousness. At the swimming-baths, Sally had been the most talkative and noisy of the girls. Now, as she moved stealthily forward towards the barn, no one could have been quieter. Angela marvelled.

"He's there all right," Sally whispered, as they entered the barn.

It took Angela some time to see what Sally had seen. Then she, too, saw the owl, apparently sleeping in a crevice just under the eaves of the barn.

The girls moved forward silently, and were able to make out the speckled plumage of a tawny owl. As they watched him, he opened his eyes, only once, almost as if he were winking at them, and then relapsed into sleep.

On the way home they talked about wildflowers. Sally challenged Angela to think of plants and flowers linked with the names of animals.

"Harebell, foxglove, cowslip, bulrush, lambstail—" began Sally.

"Dog-rose, dandelion, tiger lily, catmint, henbane," said Angela, and then broke off, as Sally said she could hear a woodpecker drumming.

For a better look, they turned off the lane. Angela was delighted to see the red head and black-and-white body of a woodpecker.

"Bother, there's someone coming! He'll frighten it away!" said Sally.

Angela took a quick look at the approaching figure in the distance and said hastily: "It's that man Benson again—you know, the man who owns Four Oaks. Don't let him see us, for goodness' sake."

They slipped through a gap in the hedge as Benson drew near. He passed them without seeing them. When they thought it safe, they followed him cautiously. They were easily able to keep him in sight without being seen. At a tumbledown cottage, Benson stopped, then went in.

"Mrs. Turley lives there," Sally told Angela. "She's been the talk of the village. She's come in for some money. I hope Benson hasn't got designs on it."

"I wouldn't put anything past him from what I've seen of him," said Angela grimly.

That evening Angela attended the Guides' barbecue. Afterwards, she and Margaret went round to hear Judy's pop records. It was quite dark when they set off for home. Margaret lived in the same direction as Jessamine Cottage. They took a path which led first across fields and then through a wood.

"There can't be far to go now," said Angela presently. She was beginning to feel tired. "I suppose we must be somewhere near Four Oaks."

Suddenly, Margaret stopped. "Listen! I believe there's someone coming. I shouldn't like to meet Benson at this time of night. Let's keep quiet and out of sight."

It was a clear night, and a patch of moonlight lit up a point where two paths met. As the two Guides drew back into the shadow of a big tree,

"It's Benson!" breathed Angela

the footsteps they had heard came nearer. Every now and then there was the noise of snapping twigs.

"Whoever it is, is carrying something heavy," whispered Margaret.

A man stepped into the clearing.

"It's Benson!" breathed Angela.

They waited until the man had got well out of earshot, and then Margaret said: "Did you see what he was carrying—planks!"

"Why in the world would anybody be carrying planks about at midnight?" remarked Angela.

"It isn't midnight, but I know what you mean."

When they reached the garden of Four Oaks, Margaret crossed to the fence.

"He went in the house, but he didn't put the light on. Whatever he's doing, he's keeping it dark!"

Angela's mother had invited the Kingfishers to tea. Angela spent the whole of the next morning in the kitchen with her mother. She was determined

They slipped through a gap in the hedge and watched

to show the local Guides that though they could beat her hollow in country lore she could cook. She had gained the Cook badge.

She did have the satisfaction of seeing every crumb of her cake eaten.

"It's simply super!" Margaret told her, and Sally nodded with her mouth full.

They played games until even Sally was exhausted. Margaret told the Guides of the strange behaviour of Benson the previous night. Sally offered her own interpretation of the affair. There was some dark secret buried under the floor of the cottage, she told them. It could be loot from a robbery. It might even be a body!

"The Kingfishers," declared Sally, "ought to do something about such sinister happenings."

"Perhaps if we blackened our faces and crept up to the cottage window one night we might see what Benson is up to," suggested Judy.

"Your face is usually so dirty it wouldn't need blacking," Liz teased.

"I'm worried about Benson having dealings with Mrs. Turley," said Margaret thoughtfully. "He would know she's come into money and may be trying to get her to part with it. Perhaps he's persuaded her to buy Four Oaks for a lot more than it's worth."

"Tell you what," said Judy; "while you play another game, I'll go round to Mrs. Turley and see if I can find out anything from her. I know her quite well, and I'm a bit concerned for her."

When Judy returned, she looked serious.

"It's as bad as we thought," she said. "Mrs. Turley is going to buy Four Oaks."

"No!" cried Margaret.

"We ought to stop it!" cried Sally.

"How can we?" asked Angela. "Besides, why shouldn't Mrs. Turley buy it if she wants to?"

"Because Benson's the seller, that's why," replied Judy grimly.

"The time has come," said Margaret solemnly, "for the Kingfishers to take a hand."

"Agreed," said Judy, "but we only suspect that Benson will in some way diddle Mrs. Turley. We've got no proof, and we've no idea how unless it is that he's selling Four Oaks at an inflated price."

"Somehow I've got the feeling that there's more to it than that," Angela put in. "What's he doing dragging planks around with him in the dark of the night?"

"There's only one way to find out," declared Sally—"go and see."

Judy nodded thoughtfully. "Four Oaks isn't far away, and there's no time like the present. How

One by one the Guides peered through the slit into the lighted room

about sallying round and peeping in through the windows?"

"Here's one that'll sally," said Sally. "Her name's Sally."

"Come on, then!"

The other Guides were ready to leave, so the four said goodbye and then made their way to Four Oaks.

"Benson's in there!" breathed Margaret. "He's got a light on."

The window through which a very thin chink of light came was at the side of the house. There was a split in the blind that had been drawn over the window, and one by one the Guides peered through it. Not all the room could be seen, but Benson was visible. He appeared to be pulling up floorboards near the open hearth. The planks Angela and Margaret had seen him carrying the previous night were standing up in a corner of the room.

"It looks as if he's replacing floorboards," remarked Margaret. "Nothing sinister in that."

"Isn't there?" said Judy. "I'm not so sure. I'd love to get inside and check."

"What have you got in mind?" asked Sally curiously. "I know a way we might get inside—if we're brave enough to take a risk."

"How?"

"Make a noise. Benson will come out to investigate, and while he's looking round the outside we'll slip in through the door and hide."

Angela drew a deep breath. "Dare we?"

"I'd dare," Sally stated calmly.

"So would I," added Judy. "It's a good idea, Sally. Of course we might have to wait a long time in there, but he's bound to finish what he's doing sooner or later and then we'd be free to investigate."

Swiftly she outlined a plan. Angela and Margaret were to be decoys. When Benson had been lured away from the door from which he would go to find out the cause of the noise the two Guides would make, Judy and Sally would slip in and hide in the house. The other two would then keep watch until Benson left the house, and then Judy and Sally would let them in, and all four would try and find the solution to the riddle of Four Oaks.

Angela and Margaret decoyed Benson out of the house by the simple expedient of knocking on the front door and then slipping round to the back of the house. Judy and Sally crouched in the bushes near the front door. When Benson opened the door and found no one there, he walked down the steps and looked round. Seeing no sign of anyone, he was about to return indoors when Angela, watching from a vantage-point stamped her feet loudly on the path. Benson ran round the side of the house to investigate. Angela made herself scarce, and Judy and Sally grasped the opportunity and slipped into the house through the open door.

Muttering to himself, Benson made his way back and into the house.

There followed what seemed to Angela and Margaret an interminable wait. They realised it must be worse for the two Guides inside, who wouldn't dare to move about for fear of revealing their presence to Benson.

At long last, however, Benson finished his work near the fireplace and gathered up the tools he had been using. Switching off the light, he left by the front door, which he locked behind him.

"Thank goodness!" breathed Judy. "I don't think I could have waited much longer."

"I was almost ready to scream," admitted Sally. "Now let's open the door for the others—if they're still there."

Angela and Margaret were still there, but, as Angela explained, they hadn't stayed in one spot.

"We had to," Judy pointed out. "We're stiff and cramped and fed up."

"Have a piece of choc," offered Margaret, and the two gratefully accepted.

They went into the room in which Benson had been working.

Judy walked over to the fireplace. "My dad's a builder, and he's told me what he looks for in old houses like this one—woodworm and dry rot—and I'll bet that's what Four Oaks has got." She knelt down and examined the floorboards near the new ones let in by Benson. Then, on hands and knees, she prowled round the room scrutinising the floor. "That's it!" she announced triumphantly. "Benson's selling Mrs. Turley a place riddled with woodworm and dry rot. He's covered up the worst, but I bet the whole house is rotten with it."

Judy knelt down and peered at the floorboards

"So that's why he works at night and stops people looking over the house!"

"The fact is," said Judy grimly, "an innocent old lady like Mrs. Turley wouldn't bother to call in a surveyor to report on the state of the house, whereas other buyers would; that's why Benson took care not to let the agents send house-hunters in and sold the place to newly rich Mrs. Turley."

"Guides," said Margaret, "I think we've done a good night's work."

"I feel I've earned every penny of what I'm not going to get," declared Sally.

"We shall save poor Mrs. Turley's pennies, which is the main thing," said Judy.

The following morning all four Guides called on Mrs. Turley and explained what they had discovered. Mrs. Turley was shocked and very grateful. She was very keen on becoming the owner of Four Oaks, but in view of the Guides' exposure of the deception Benson had tried to practise she felt like withdrawing from the purchase. On further thought, however, she asked Judy to ask her father to call on her, as she wanted him to make a thorough survey of the house and give her an estimate for eliminating the woodworm and dry rot.

The Guides learned the outcome of it all later through Judy, who reported that Benson was furious on learning that at the last minute Mrs. Turley wanted a survey made. At first he refused to allow it, but on Mrs. Turley's stating that she would go no further with the purchase until the house was surveyed he gave way. Judy's father duly reported on the condition of the house and submitted an estimate for putting it to rights. Mrs. Turley thereupon deducted the amount of the estimate from the price she had been willing to pay for the house, and Benson, enraged but impotent, had no course but to accept in order to achieve a sale without incurring the expense himself of having the woodworm and dry rot corrected or of paying an agent commission.

Mrs. Turley wanted to reward the Guides for what they had done, but they all declined. The grateful lady, however, insisted on donating a handsome sum to the Company's funds, which ensured a summer camp for the whole Company the following year, plus Angela, who was cordially invited.

"It's been a good holiday," Angela confided to her mother when the time came for them to leave Jessamine Cottage, "the best ever, I think."

"It might have been less successful if you hadn't joined up with Guides here," said her mother.

"And got mixed up in the strange affair of Four Oaks," grinned Angela.

The 24-Hour Clock

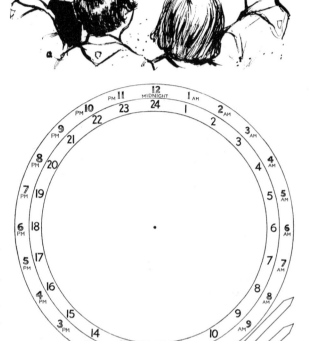

Every Guide should be able to tell the time as readily by the twenty-four-hour clock as by the twelve-hour one. To make sure that all the members of your Patrol are proficient in reading the twenty-four-hour clock, make one and test their proficiency with it.

Make the clock as shown in the drawing in cardboard. Cut out two fingers and fasten them in the centre with a push-through paper-clip.

The second drawing indicates how the minutes of the twenty-four-hour clock are shown between each hour.

Check yourself and your Patrol by calling out times in the old way and then writing down how they would be shown on the twenty-four-hour clock, thus:

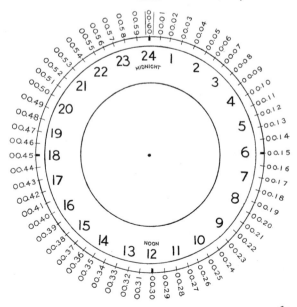

OLD CLOCK		24-HOUR CLOCK
A	8-30 a.m.	
B	9-15 a.m.	
C	12-05 p.m.	
D	8-45 p.m.	
E	4-20 a.m.	
F	1-00 p.m.	
G	8-30 p.m.	
H	11-40 p.m.	
I	7-10 a.m.	
J	2-20 p.m.	

ANSWERS

A	08.30	F	13.00
B	09.15	G	20.30
C	12.05	H	23.40
D	20.45	I	07.10
E	04.20	J	14.20

Make a Tree-Board

For a Guiding Exhibition or for Your Patrol Home

by Sydney R. Brown

Have you ever made a tree-board? This makes an interesting pastime for summer camp. The tree-board can be kept for reference purposes and study

during the winter months. Mount as many examples as possible of trees on a sheet of hardboard or three-ply.

On each board glue samples of a tree's bark, leaves, fruit or berries. Surround these with sketches or photographs of the tree itself. Add notes on where the type of tree can be found and what use can be made of its wood for fires, furniture, etc., and you have an instructive board, perhaps covering a number of camps.

An aspect of trees useful for Guides to know is the value of their woods for fires, though of course Guides don't look on

trees merely as firewood! Soft wood will always burn away quickly, but is very useful for starting a fire. Two dry sticks with upward cuts made in them with a knife, leaving shavings sticking out rather like a miniature Christmas tree, will act as tinder if stuck into the ground side by side and covered with thin, dry twigs.

The best woods for camp cooking are from the ash, apple, beech, birch, maple and sycamore. Chestnut, elm, poplar and willow burn badly. Nothing can beat birchbark for fire-lighting, but it should never be peeled off a living tree. You can usually find some lying at the foot of a tree, or take some from a dead branch.

Notes in this strain on your tree-board will add to its interest and usefulness.

RED-INDIAN-STYLE PATROL NOTICE-BOARD

YOU CAN MAKE IT

1. THE RED INDIANS EXCELLED AT CURING BUFFALO SKINS. AN IMITATION OF A SKIN

MAKES AN ATTRACTIVE AND UNUSUAL NOTICE-BOARD.

2. THE HIDE MIGHT BE CUT TO SHAPE FROM A PIECE OF LEATHER OR SKIVER.

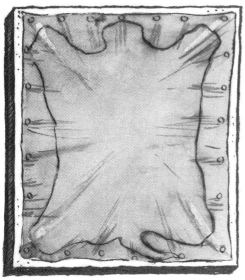

3. ANOTHER METHOD IS TO SOAK A SHEET OF STRONG WRAPPING-PAPER IN A BOWL OF WARM WATER.

4. SQUEEZE OUT THE WATER AND PIN THE PAPER ON A FLAT BOARD. WHEN IT IS DRY, DRAW THE OUTLINE OF THE SKIN. ADD THE MARKINGS IN BRIGHT COLOURS, THEN CUT OUT.

5. THE FRAME IS MADE OF SELECTED BRANCHES FROM TREES, LASHED AT EACH CORNER. MOUNT THE HIDE ON THE FRAME WITH CORDS. FINALLY GIVE THE WHOLE THING A COAT OF VARNISH.

Friezes for Fun

by T. A. Cochrane

You don't need a lot of things to start making friezes for fun. To begin with, you need a strip of shelf-paper about 4ft. long and 18ins. to 2ft. deep; some poster paints in red, blue, yellow, white and black; a paintbrush; a pot of paste and a pastebrush; scissors; scraps of coloured papers or materials; and a pencil.

Now you have to decide what your frieze is going to be about. The seaside is a good subject to start with, and you can have fun putting in all the things you like to see by the sea.

Our frieze is 5ft. long and 2ft. deep. The first thing we did was to work out where the sand and sea would be, and we drew them in roughly. On the right-hand side we sketched some rocks. From the rocks the sand stretched to the bottom left-hand corner, and a wavy line showed where the sea was.

We painted the sky pale-blue, and while it was drying we coloured the sand yellow. Then we did the deep-blue sea and the rocks, which were grey. Lastly we painted white wavelets on the sea. You have to be sure that one colour is dry before you paint on another colour next to it.

While you wait for the last paint to dry you can be deciding on what else you're going to put on your frieze. You can have as little or as much on as you want. Whenever we think of the sea we think of boats, so we found some brown paper and cut out a boat shape, which we stuck on the sea. We added some smart white paper sails and a little man that we cut out from an advertisement to sit in her. Then we cut out some silver-paper fishes to jump out of the water. When we'd stuck these down we painted in ripples with white paint. On the rocks we pasted seaweedy shapes made out of dark-green cloth. We also tried to draw a crab, but as it didn't look very much like a crab we hunted through all the old "comics" we had until we found a really good picture of one. This we cut out and stuck on the sandy part of the frieze. While we were looking for the crab we found a picture of a girl and boy playing

with a beach-ball, so we cut them out and pasted them into place, adding a bucket and spade, a starfish and some shells.

Last of all, we cut out some seagulls from white paper. These are quite easy to do, as you can see from the sketch. You have to cut out a curved piece of paper with the points facing in opposite directions, stick a paper "body" to the middle of it, and then bend the bottom

wing upwards. Make as many as you need.

Of course, we could have added a lot more things, but it's best not to overload a frieze with too much detail.

There are all sorts of subjects which make exciting friezes—a Guide camp, bonfire night, Christmas snow scenes, underwater pictures, jungles, etc. Why not try creating an effective frieze for your Patrol home or for the Guide hall?

HIKE TOOLS FOR CAMPING AND HIKING

Before the spring arrives, with its inviting sunny days calling you to be out and about, be prepared! Make these tools in readiness for hikes.

First make a collection of strong wire. Cheap wire coat-hangers are excellent

for this job. Then ask Daddy to lend you his wire-cutters and pincers or pliers, and set to work to make the following:

A. For your Dampers. B. Toasting Fork. C. Pothook, for hanging your small dixie or billycan over the fire. D. For toasting your cheese-dreams—this needs a wooden handle bound on, a chance to use your whipping knowledge. E. This is a griller. Cut a square piece of tin and hammer it flat. Then with your pliers bend a rim down each edge and hammer it flat over the prongs of your fork. Bind on a wooden handle, a s for your cheese-dream toaster.

The Slim and Svelte Patrol

by Rikki Taylor

could suggest some gorgeous menus, but they're all so fattening."

The other Kingfishers nodded in agreement.

"At summer camp I gained three-quarters of a stone," groaned Tess, whose plump figure could not really afford to gain an ounce. She added unhappily: "It only took a week to put on, but I've dieted for a month, and only managed to lose a pound."

The Kingfishers all knew how easy it

The Kingfishers sprawled on the short grass in the park. Each member of the Patrol had a face creased with deep lines of concentrated thought, for they had gathered to discuss a most important matter—FOOD.

Jan, the P.L., while plucking viciously at some inoffensive blades of grass, explained.

"During this weekend camp, which runs from Friday evening until Monday afternoon, each Patrol will do its own cooking. Thank goodness we can use butane gas! But we must plan our own menus."

Phil, the Second, sighed deeply. "I

was to gain weight, especially at camp, where appetites soar in the fresh air and the menu is inclined to have a high proportion of starchy food.

"It's the potatoes," sighed Mary, another plump Kingfisher.

"And the thick slices of white bread," added Phil.

"Thick, sweet chocolate too," sighed Tess; "but one must eat and drink *something*."

Jan, always practical, brought them down to the truth.

"It's the money, you mean," she stated flatly. "We *could* live on steaks and asparagus tips and fresh peaches and scampi. We *could* plan a good, healthy menu with very little starch content, but —oh!—it *would* be pricy."

But the Kingfishers concentrated on the problem of finding the right menu, and finally they produced it. It was balanced, exciting, not too pricy, and with that international dash approved in the higher grades of cuisine. Above all, it had the minimum of filling, fattening, far-from-flattering starch. Here it is.

Friday—Supper—French
Packeted onion soup, with grated cheese sprinkled on top of each bowl just before serving.

Saturday—Breakfast—Hungarian
Halved grapefruit or orange, scrambled eggs, sausage and bacon. Slice each of wholemeal bread. Tea or coffee.
Cut one slice of bacon and ¼lb. sausages in small pieces, and fry lightly in a little fat. Break 6 eggs, add seasoning and mix with a fork. Add the cooked bacon and sausage cubes. Heat a little butter in a pan, and drop in sufficient of the mixture for two people, cooking it until brown on each side.

Saturday—Dinner—American
Meat balls with vegetables. Fresh fruit salad and custard.
Add one beaten egg and seasoning to 1lb. minced steak. Form into 6 balls. Fry with one diced onion in very little fat until balls are brown. Pour off any remaining fat. Add one large can of concentrated vegetable-soup and one pint of water. Simmer slowly for as long as possible. Serve with carrots, cooked separately.

Saturday—Tea—French
Tomato and cucumber salad. Wholemeal bread. Jelly and fruit juice. 1 slice of cake (if weakening).
Slice a small cucumber as finely as possible, sprinkle with salt, leave for 45 mins., then drain. Add 4 finely sliced, large tomatoes, and sprinkle with a sauce of a mixture of half lemon juice, half olive oil, and seasoning. If available, sprinkle with chopped parsley. Leave to stand as long as possible.

Saturday—Supper—American
Crackers and cheese.

Sunday—Breakfast—Norwegian (quick, to allow time for church)
Halved grapefruit or orange. Piece of crispbread, spread with butter and cheese. Slice of wholemeal bread, spread with liver pate. Glass of milk.

Sunday—Dinner—American
Chicken Maryland, with green beans. Tinned grapefruit sprinkled with chopped, unsalted nuts.
Cut a small roasting chicken into 6 joints. Coat each with egg and breadcrumbs. Fry in ½" of fat (at first quickly) to brown, and then slowly until tender. Drain, and serve with fried halves of bananas, watercress or lettuce, and tinned green beans.

Sunday—Tea—British
Boiled eggs. Wholemeal bread. Jam. Cake (if weakening).

Sunday—Supper—South American
Beef tea (from cubes or concentrated extract). Crackers.

Monday—Breakfast—Chinese
Halved grapefruit or orange. Savoury omelette. 1 slice wholemeal bread.. Tea or coffee.
Chop finely and mix together 4ozs. lean bacon or ham and a small onion. Add any left-over nuts or vegetables, chopped. Beat 5 eggs and seasoning, and add the other ingredients. Drop spoonfuls into hot fat, frying for approx. 10 minutes.

Monday—Dinner—Austrian
Beef goulash and cabbage. Cheese, crackers and apple.
Thinly slice 1lb. onions and fry in a little fat until golden-brown. Cut a large tin of corned beef into pieces, and add this to the onions, with seasoning, plus a tin of tomato pulp. Serve with boiled cabbage.

Well, as you will have gathered, the

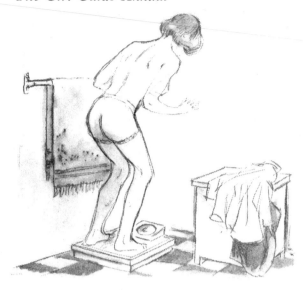

Kingfishers ate royally. As they folded their tents, Phil sighed regretfully.

"I wish we were just coming. It's all been super, and the non-fattening food was fab!"

But Tess had her own reasons for wanting to get home. As soon as she entered the house she dumped her kit in the hall, dashed up to her bedroom, kicked off her shoes, pulled off her uniform, and stepped on to the scales.

"I've LOST—I've actually LOST two pounds in weight!" she whooped.

"Have you been starving yourself?" asked her anxious mother.

For answer Tess took a full purse from her shoulder-bag.

"I didn't spend a penny at the tuck-shop, or on any extra food. I just didn't want it." Then, with great pride, she showed her mother a pennant. "The Kingfishers' non-fattening diet must have provided plenty of energy," she said triumphantly. "We won the camp competition."

WHICH PATROL FOR SALLY?

Sally is going up to Guides from Brownies. Which Patrol is she joining? To find out, draw the shapes in the frames below into the blank frames with the corresponding numbers.

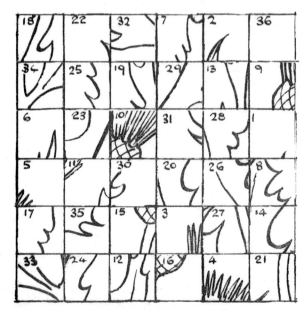

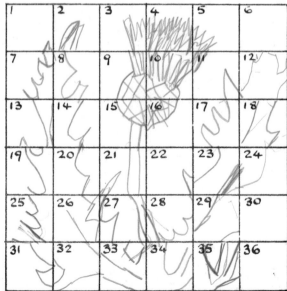

THISTLES

CAMP AND CORNER TIDY

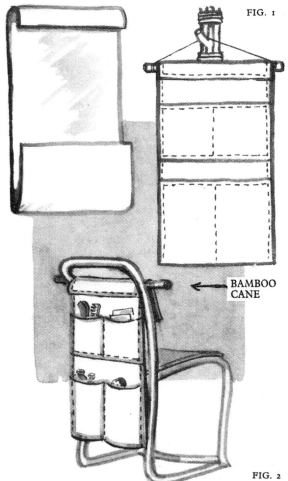

FIG. 1

BAMBOO CANE

FIG. 2

Here is a useful tidy to make in readiness for camp. It will be most useful for your Patrol corner, too.

You need an oddment of strong material; about half a yard 36″ wide is sufficient. Hem this strip down both sides, and turn down a wide hem at the top, leaving the ends open.

Turn up a deep hem at the bottom to form two pockets; hem the edge before stitching the sides in place.

Now you will need another strip of material to fit across the top, as shown in the sketch (Fig. 1), dividing this into two or three pockets, as you wish. This is your basic tidy, and in camp you push a suitable piece of wood through the top hem, fasten a piece of hooked wood to the tent pole, and hang it on this. It will now take your hairbrush and comb, your writing paper and pen, your metal polish, and other oddments.

For your Patrol home, you can use a short bamboo cane and hang it up on the back of a chair, as shown in Fig. 2.

"Do you have to feed the birds at five a.m.?"

HINT FOR HOSTESSES

Flavoured milk drinks will be relished by your Patrol members or other friends who visit you in your home. To make, mix about a third of a cup of fruit-juice and syrup with a cupful of chilled milk. Mix until frothy and add sugar to taste.

71

What is your favourite tree? Is it the sturdy oak? Is it the graceful birch, the stately cedar, the beautiful weeping willow?

Here's a charming poem about the weeping willow by Aileen E. Passmore:

I've never seen the willow weep
But I know it does, for, oh!
There's a pool of quiet water
Shining silver down below—
A pool filled with the cool sweet tears
The willow's wept throughout the years.

"Only God

Says the Editor

I think my own favourite tree is the poplar. As I look out of my window I can see a row of poplars. Each one is stately and graceful, aloof from earthly things as it aspires to the heavens. Branches upturned in prayer, these poplars seem to spend their days and years in quiet contemplation of clouds and stars and sky.

You know Joyce Kimer's poem "Trees", don't you? It was set to music many years ago.

Can Make A Tree"

TREES

I think that I shall never see
A poem lovely as a tree.
A tree whose hungry mouth is prest
Against the earth's sweet-flowing breast;
A tree that looks at God all day,
And lifts her leafy arms to pray;
A tree that may in summer wear
A nest of robins in her hair;
Upon whose bosom snow has lain;
Who intimately lives with rain.
Poems are made by fools like me,
But only God can make a tree.

Can you identify the trees on these two pages?

Buch

Cedar

Willow

Recently, men cut down about ten elm-trees bordering the meadow near my house. It was a sad sight. How long it took for those tall trees to grow, and how quickly their end came! Now the rooks must seek another home, and I must avert my eyes from the gap that's left.

Let's cherish our beautiful trees and woods, remembering that they can be cut down in a day or an hour but take a human lifetime to grow to full glory.

On the day that you made your Guide Promise I wonder if you thought of the millions of boys and girls, men and women, all around the world who have made the same Promise, and of the millions before them in the years since Baden-Powell founded the Scout and Guide Movement at the beginning of this century.

The ideals expressed in that Promise remain the same, although the actual words may differ according to the language and the historical background of the people of the country or community. For instance, a member of *Les Guides de France* would say (in French, of course):

> On my honour and with the grace of God I pledge myself
>> To do my best to serve God, the church and my country,
>> To help others in all circumstances,
>> To observe the Guide Law.

Another Association includes service to the family, and yet another promises "To be a real Guide".

In the United States a Girl Scout begins with the words,

> On my honour I will try: To do my duty to God . . .

Is there a difference between "I will try" and "I will do my best"? That is a talking point for your Patrol. Here are some others: A few years ago the Promise for Guides of the United Kingdom was changed from the one that had been used for many years. To begin with, the words "on my honour" were omitted. It was argued that "A promise is a promise and the words 'on my honour' do not make it any more binding." What do you think?

"To do my duty . . . to the Queen" became "To serve the Queen" and was transferred from the first to the second part of the Promise and linked with "help other people", while "at all times" was omitted.

Now we come to the Law. The comparison with the "old" Law is even more interesting. To take just one example, consider the original 9th Law, "A Guide is thrifty". That word "thrifty" has in the course of time become old-fashioned and today may even suggest meanness. So now we have two Laws to take its place, the 8th and 9th, because in spite of much thought and considerable research in dictionary and thesaurus nobody could find a suitable up-to-date word to convey the true meaning of thrift. Economical comes close, but again in certain senses it could suggest meanness. Of course, one could have said "A Guide is not wasteful", but all the Laws are positive, and I am sure everyone would agree that it would have been a mistake to introduce the negative.

That excellent book *Trefoil Around the World*, which I hope you have in your Guide library, gives the Laws for all the countries that are members of the World Association of Girl Guides and Girl

Other Lands

by Alix Liddell

Scouts, and these sometimes throw a new light on our own Laws. You know, of course, that in some countries there are several Guide Associations linked in a federation and that it is this federation that represents the country as a whole in the World Association. You will notice when you study *Trefoil Around the World* that the laws of the different Associations within the same country are not always exactly alike. In the following examples I have, for the sake of brevity, given only the name of the country, and only one country at that.

"A Guide knows how to obey". This Belgian law seems to suggest that one should obey quickly and efficiently—provided that it is not against the promptings of one's conscience to do so. Sweden restricts obedience to "parents, teachers and leaders", supposing that such people would never require a girl to do anything dishonourable. "A Guide is self-disciplined" (Ivory Coast) describes another form of obedience, but might also refer to our 10th Law.

In Dahomey (do you know where that is, by the way?) a Guide is "generous; she is prepared to help" and also "welcoming; she has the team spirit"; in France she "likes to work and does not fear endeavour, does nothing by halves"; in Cyprus she is "reliable and punctual", thus making the best use of her own and other people's time; in the Netherlands she "bears disappointment with a smile", surely a way of showing courage and cheerfulness in difficult circumstances; and again in France she "listens to others and respects their convictions". I wonder to which of our Laws you would compare this. I could mention many more, but I shall leave you to discover them for yourself.

During the last ten years or so the wind of change has been blowing strongly through the great world, and Guiding has not been unaffected. Numbers of countries have changed their programmes and reworded their Promise and Law, and others are still in the process of doing so. Guiding does not stand still. If your Patrol were asked now to draw up ten Laws what would they be? Why not have a go? It may be more difficult than you think!

The best thing about Guiding, to my mind, is that we have friends in almost every part of the free world, all holding the same beliefs as expressed in the Promise and Law, and all eager to welcome us to their homelands, just as we are eager to welcome them should they come to our country, whether on a visit or to settle here.

THE CANTANKEROUS OLD HARRIDAN

by ETHEL WALTER

"I—I came to see you, Grandma"

Gillian was delighted when Grandma moved into a flat in Gilpin Street.

"Granny's such fun," she said.

Daddy looked up from his morning paper. "Fun? When she stayed with Aunt Jennifer after her operation, Aunt Jennifer called her a cantankerous old harridan."

Mother passed the marmalade. "You could look in on her after school, Gillian, instead of waiting here alone for us to come from work. As for her being fun—well!"

"If she isn't," Gillian declared, "it'll be because she's had to leave lovely Seabourne. It must be horrid to be old and ill."

"Her Seabourne house was far too large for one person," Daddy explained.

Gillian frowned as she hurried for the bus. Cantankerous old harridan indeed! Grandma was a love, with her white hair, blue eyes and pink cheeks.

But when Gillian called after school she found that, although Grandma's hair was still white and her eyes blue, her cheeks were no longer pink and her mouth was harder.

"Hullo!" the old lady grumbled. "Has somebody left the lid off your dustbin?"

Gillian's eyes widened. "I don't know. Why?"

"I wondered how you managed to blow this way."

Was Grandma joking? But she seemed serious enough.

"I—I—I came to see you, Grandma."

"Why? I don't suppose you want to tell me, though. Shut the door before anything else drifts in." As she led the way to the kitchen she asked, "Have you had your tea?"

Gillian shook her head.

"Well, I have, and I'm not getting the things out again."

"That's all right. I always wait until Mother and Dad come home at six o'clock."

"It's too long!" Grandma sounded so fierce that Gillian felt quite upset. But she's old and ill, she remembered, and she had to leave Seabourne.

"I wondered if I could do anything to help you," she said.

Grandma's sharp eyes flashed. "There's the washing-up, if it won't spoil your soft hands."

Gillian chuckled. Her hands were tanned because she seldom wore gloves and they were none too clean after a day at school.

"I'd love it," she said.

"H'm! Then I must find you something you'll hate."

"Cantankerous old harridan," Gillian remembered, as she ran the tap.

It hardly seemed worth the trouble. There was only a cup and saucer, a plate, a spoon and a butter knife.

"You can't have had much tea," she said.

Grandma sniffed. "So your mother's sent you to spy on me, has she? You'll tell her I don't get enough to eat."

Gillian felt tears pricking behind her eyes. Was this the grandmother who on holiday at Seabourne used to help her build sand-castles, paddle with her, collect shells and pebbles, and at night tuck her into bed and tell her wonderful bedtime stories? She must be feeling very tired and ill to be so unpleasant.

"I came because I wanted to see you," Gillian said quietly.

"And you'll go home and tell tales."

"Not if you'll mind. All the same, I wish you'd have proper meals."

"When you get to my age you won't want to be bothered with cooking."

Gillian's eyes sparkled. "I love cooking. I'm going in for the Cook badge at Guides. Would you let me come in sometimes and cook for you?"

The other was silent for so long that Gillian wondered whether she'd heard.

"You'd like to poison me, eh? Well, it's one way of getting rid of me. Come if you like, but I'd rather have somebody to make my breakfast. To have it in bed would be nice—yes, very nice."

"Give me a key and I'll come in before I go to school."

Grandma screwed up her eyes almost as though she was trying not to cry.

"Very well!" she said at last. "But first you'll need to do some shopping."

"I'll go right away. The supermarket's open until six. What would you like?"

"Use your own judgment, child. If you're going to be a home help you should do it properly. Anyway, I'm not interested in food."

She handed over her purse.

"How much shall I take? How much shall I need?"

"How should I know? Take the lot and see."

"Eggs, bacon and sausages," Gillian decided. Grandma was hungry. She needed good meals.

She let herself into Grandma's flat at seven o'clock next morning. She put on the kettle. She'd make a cup of tea first. She laid the tray as she'd been taught, with biscuits on a pretty dish and a bunch of Daddy's sweetpeas. Everything looked so tempting that she smiled to herself as she tapped on the bedroom door.

"Come in!" Grandma sounded as cross as two sticks.

"I—I've brought you a cup of tea." Gillian's

"Why rouse me at the crack of dawn?" said Grandma

"Look at me when I'm talking to you," said Grandma

voice faltered as she met a pair of hard eyes.

"You've made a thorough commotion, enough to waken the dead. Who do you think wants to be roused at the crack of dawn?"

"But I've got to go to school, and I've still got to poach your egg and make toast."

"Egg! Toast! My dear child, this will be all the breakfast I'll need. I'm too old to stuff myself."

Gillian fiddled with the door handle. If Grandma thought she could make her cry she could jolly well think again. She swallowed the lump that was trying to choke her and forced herself to smile.

"Very well! I'll come a bit later tomorrow, but I'll call in on my way from school and make your tea."

She didn't wait for the old woman to object. She closed the bedroom door and returned to the kitchen. If she couldn't cook breakfast she could do a bit of housework. The windows needed washing, and a good dusting wouldn't do the lounge any harm.

When she went to collect the tray she found that Grandma had eaten one biscuit and drunk her tea. Now she was sleeping. Gillian tiptoed away, washed up the crocks and ran for the bus—and missed it and was late for school.

Miss Evans was angry. Life, thought Gillian, was very difficult! It was specially hard on the young!

"Coming with us, Gillian?" Diana and Wendy took her arms. "We're going to have a coke."

"I can't really stop."

"Oh, come on! We want to talk about that dance the Scouts are getting up."

"All right," said Gillian, "but I must get away pretty soon. I've got to call in at my gran's."

She stayed longer than she had intended. She would have liked to stay longer still, but she tore herself away.

When at last she reached Grandma's flat, she found that Grandma had got her own tea.

"I boiled myself an egg. I thought you'd changed your mind about helping."

"She's so impatient, so unreasonable," Gillian told her parents.

"She's been ill, dear, don't forget. Perhaps we could get one of the neighbours to give her a hand."

"Don't do that, Mother. I'll carry on. I won't go quite so early, though, in future."

All through the summer, morning and evening, Gillian called in at Grandma's flat. Grandma made no secret of her belief that she'd tire of the task.

"But at least she eats what I cook now," Gillian reported to her parents.

The Cantankerous Old Harridan

Gillian's eyes misted with tears

"But Aunt Jennifer says Grandma's still a cantankerous old harridan," her mother said, smiling.

Gillian giggled. "Grandma says Aunt Jennifer tries to manage her, and she'd rather manage herself, thank you."

"Does she never get cantankerous with you?"

Gillian gave a rueful smile. "Doesn't she just! But I don't answer back. I just say to myself, 'Poor Gran. She's old and ill and she had to leave Seabourne—it's no wonder she's cantankerous.' And you know, Mother, she's not as thin as she was. She even does some of her own cleaning. She says I fuss too much and that I ought to be swimming or playing tennis, not playing at keeping house."

"She must be feeling better. You'll have to give her a miss on Saturday when you go on your Guide outing to Seabourne."

"I'm not going."

"Not going? But you've paid your fare and everything. Why ever not?"

"They're leaving at eight o'clock. Grandma likes her breakfast at a quarter past."

"Surely she could make her own for once?"

"I haven't told Gran about it. It would only make her more cantankerous than ever."

"You're three minutes late," the old woman snapped when Gillian took in her tray.

Gillian plumped up the old lady's pillows, but did not answer. Silence was her best defence.

"And yesterday my egg was hard. You know I like eggs lightly cooked. And what's this—haddock? I'll be thirsty as a fish all day. And I'd like coffee instead of tea occasionally."

Gillian fiddled with the curtains, pretending to look out of the window. She couldn't see anything; her eyes were misted with tears.

Cantankerous old harridan! To think she'd missed her day at the seaside for somebody who could do nothing but complain!

"Look at me, child, when I'm talking to you."

Gillian blinked, swallowed hard and turned. Grandma stared at her over her tea-cup. All of a sudden, her spectacles misted over and her mouth trembled. "Gillian, my dear, why do you never tell me anything?"

Gillian blinked her surprise at the altered tone.

"Wh—what do you mean, Grandma?"

"I know people say things about me. What is it they say? I want to know. Speak up, child! What do they say about me?"

"They call you a cantankerous old harridan," Gillian blurted out, and then clapped a hand to her mouth.

Grandma threw back her white head and laughed and laughed.

"A cantankerous old harridan! That's rich!" All of a sudden she was fierce again. "Why didn't you tell me you'd booked to go on a Guide outing?"

"It started too early for me to get your breakfast as well."

"You stupid little goose! Off you go! Get into your uniform and be back here in half an hour. Aunt Jennifer is taking me to Seabourne. You're coming too. We'll be there as soon as the coach, and you'll be able to join your friends."

"But—but—"

Grandma gave a funny sort of chuckle. "My poor pet! I must have driven you crazy. I'm not really the pest I must have seemed—not now I'm so much better. I'm better because of what you've done for me. Oh, yes, I am. It isn't only that you've got meals for me. You've been company for me and you've been kind. And that's what I needed more than anything—company and kindness. I shan't forget what you've done for me, Gillian. You're a real Guide. I've got a flat at Seabourne. I'm going back there as soon as it's ready, and I hope you'll spend some of your holiday with me."

"Oh, Grandma, I'm so glad!"

"A cantankerous old harridan, child—that's me —or was me. Not now, though. I'm better—quite my old self, in fact—thanks to you!"

CAMP MUSINGS

CAMP HAZARDS

by Jean Howard

Did no one ever tell you
When you first arrived at camp
That it's not the early rising
Or the spiders or the damp
That causes most discomfort,
Even worse than getting cramp?

No, it's finding that your neighbour
Snores her head off every night
And that rustlings in the grasses
Wake you in a ghastly fright,
And the bumps on which you're lying
Make the dawn a welcome sight!

THE MOTH

by Jean Kenward

Snapping like a split nut
Against the light—
Look, she will break her wing!

Is it the heat or brilliance
That invites
Such febrile journeying?

Open the door—
The mild and airy dark
Will guide her wavering flight

Where is no fierce or vain
Idolatry,
But softness and sweet night.

GEOG. YOUR MEMORY

For Irish Guides

by J. W. Gosden

1. Why is Eire so dimly lit?
   Because it has its Wick-low.
2. How much did Lough Erne?
   As much as Lough Oughter (in Co. Cavan, Eire).
3. How long was Kilbeggan (West Meath)?
   As long as Kildare.
4. Why are the Western Ireland hounds noisier than the Eastern?
   Because there are more "bays".
5. Which rick would look funny in a farmyard?
   Lime-rick.
6. Why is Eire getting rich quickly?
   Because its capital (wealth) is Dublin (doublin').
7. What did Ulster reply to Leinster when she asked him to move up a bit?
   Connaught (Cannot).
8. What keeps Eire from spilling over?
   Its Cork.

INSECTIQUIZ

Can you answer the following questions correctly with a TRUE or a FALSE?

1. The lives of some mayflies last as long as from breakfast to teatime.
2. The dragonfly is a pest with a sting. Swat it!
3. The spider is not an insect but a relation of the crab.
4. A grasshopper's mouth is used for eating and not for breathing and chirping.
5. When a bee is angry it rolls its eyes.
6. When a vein in a moth's wing is damaged, it bleeds.
7. The butterfly has scales to cover and colour the whole of its body.
8. Gnats hear with their feelers (antennae).
9. Houseflies bite most in muggy weather.
10. When the queen ant dies, the workers take her outside. and bury her.
    —J.W.G.

JOHN SWEET

GLAD AND GAY

the Giddy Guides

by Eileen Chivers

Gabrielle and Gladys say,
"Our friends all call us Glad and Gay."

SUMMER CAMP

The Guides have camped for many summers,
But this year there are two newcomers.
Glad and Gay are in the throng,
So Be Prepared for what goes wrong!

On the day that they are cooks
They're favoured with some dubious looks.
Their leader says reluctantly,
"I'll leave you two to make the tea."

The twenty Guides sit on the ground,
And bread and cakes are handed round.
When Beaver starts to pour the tea,
It's just as weak as weak can be.

The friends once more prove inefficient;
They thought one teabag was sufficient!
But though the others can't stop laughing,
Our two don't mind good-natured chaffing.

At campfire on the final night
It's fancy dress—oh, what a sight!
A gipsy and an Indian squaw,
The Loch Ness monster and lots more.

Gladys simply wears a sack,
With TEABAG pinned upon her back.
And Gabrielle, not to be outdone,
Is POLLY PUT THE KETTLE ON.

Both of them for these strange guises
Are given consolation prizes,
For though no good at making tea,
They both show ingenuity!

WILY WHIP WEASEL

Wily Whip Weasel
Lives under the wood,
And I wouldn't mind betting
He's up to no good.
There's something odd
In the way he looks,
Like a criminal in
Detective books;
And the poor, silly rabbits
Whisper "What?
Is he a friend
Or is he not?"
Wily Whip Weasel
Gets no thinner
And he doesn't eat pudding
For breakfast or dinner.

by

Jean Kenward

The speed he moves at
Is quite fantastic;
Lissom and looped
Like a piece of elastic,
Smooth as treacle,
He's calculating
Who to trick next
In his hunting and hating,
Who to entice
To his bright, white trap.
"Look out!" cries blackbird.
"Watch that chap!
He's got no conscience,
He's got no shame:
Wily Whip Weasel—
That's his name."

PRESERVE THOSE SPRING FLOWERS

Don't let those bright spring flowers disappear after a few short weeks. Keep them for the rest of the year.

All you need is some thin white card, clear, sticky-backed plastic, and fresh spring flowers. Select a variety of blooms and leaves, but try to obtain the thinner types. Keep them fresh in a vase of water until you are ready to use them.

Next cut a piece of card to a size of your choice, but make sure the sticky plastic is large enough to cover the card with about an inch to spare. Arrange some petals and leaves on the card. A useful hint is to overlap some of the petals to make the overall effect more attractive. Then cut a piece of sticky-backed plastic so that it is about an inch wider than the card.

Then, starting from one end of the card, press the sticky-backed plastic down firmly (see diagram). You may find it a help if you practise this on some small pieces first. Before you fold the excess piece of plastic over, cut off the corners, as shown in the middle diagram.

This method may also be used for preserving other interesting Nature specimens. **—A.J.S.**

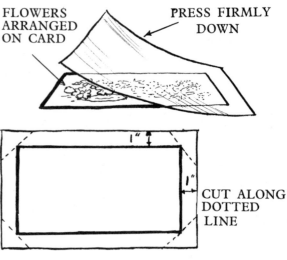

FLOWERS ARRANGED ON CARD

PRESS FIRMLY DOWN

1"

1"

CUT ALONG DOTTED LINE

FINISHED PANEL

ONCE A GUIDE, ALWAYS A GUIDE

Says JOAN DUNN, who recalls her Guiding days of fifty years ago, when she was JOAN DENISON

This phrase passed through my mind when on a bleak Saturday afternoon I answered the door-bell. There on the step stood a Guider. She wanted to know whether her small Company could use the front meadow for camp-fire lighting and other activities. They had come by bus from the nearby town.

My thoughts then went back to the day I passed a firelighting test fifty years ago, using one match.

Now and again, I watched the Guides from the window. Their blue uniforms and yellow ties made a bright contrast to the grey sky and colourless grass.

Little puffs of smoke in many directions and trips to the hedgerow for more fuel ended with a big camp-fire, and, I suppose, a sing-song. It certainly made my day. It took my mind back to my happy Guiding days.

I was twelve years old when I joined the

small village Company fifty years ago. I was proud of my secondhand uniform, which actually fitted me, and from that moment I enjoyed every meeting. We had trips in a pony and trap to other Companies. On one occasion we met at a distant school, and I passed the bedmaking test through watching others. I was not supposed to take this test on this day in a strange schoolroom.

At thirteen years of age I moved to another part of Suffolk, and my sister Kay and I joined the 1st Hintlesham Company. I was the Robin Patrol Leader and Kay the Acorn Patrol Leader. Now we really came into our own. We were so keen, and competition between us was so great, that we were kept continually on our toes. My firelighting test, some time earlier on a wet afternoon, I well remember. Eight of us

made our fires on an open pathway and a visiting Guider came to inspect them. Disaster nearly overtook mine, for just as the Guider was approaching, another Guide stepped back on to my well-laid fire. I had literally seconds in which to build it again, but I got it going and passed the test, using one match.

Other tests came quickly and the sleeve of my uniform was gaily decorated with many badges.

We really excelled at signalling, and Kay and I were chosen to practise the special message that was sent to Princess Mary when she attended a huge rally at Culfort that was attended by Guides from all around Suffolk. For weeks and weeks we joined up with other Guides to practise this message. Our marker was good, and the message we sent read something like this:

We welcome Your Highness here today.

Disaster nearly overtook the signallers, for on this important day our marker, Miss Turner, fell ill, and a new marker was chosen. When we had marched past the grandstand, we opened ranks. Our first signal from the marker was correct; then she missed the cue; but a hundred and fifty Guides without hesitation continued the well-practised message without a falter, leaving our marker with her flag still twirling when the message was finished.

All the attractions of a well-organised Rally ended with a huge singsong around an enormous camp-fire. Our Princess Royal had afternoon tea in a Guiders' marquee. We were fortunate in rescuing the flowers that adorned her table; they were a treasure for our scrapbooks.

Our Patrols, Robin and Acorn, were our greatest interest. We made close inspection of polished shoes and badges. The

Acorn Patrol had polished their Guide badges so that the G.G. on them was just a blur. The Robin Patrol excelled at swelling Guide funds, which were used for camping, etc. We made blackberry jelly from the luscious berries in the woods of our farm and sold it at fourpence a pot. We made clothes-pegs from the hazel-wood in the hedgerows. These were in demand at twopence halfpenny per dozen. They were cheap. Our fingers were sore from cutting strips of tin from used cocoa-tins.

Another money-making item was lawn handkerchieves with hand-drawn threads. These sold at threepence. Our stalls on each Whit Monday, laid out in the Rectory gardens, were eagerly attended. We were never short of funds, and contributed towards the endowing of a child's cot in the local hospital. Our other good turns were scrubbing the war memorial every so often, and tending the garden around it.

Church parade came every three months and was eagerly watched by the congregation and the younger children.

My first camp, at Orwell Park, near a river, was a long hot week packed with interest. The Jersey cows around us supplied us with milk. We had a rota of cooking days for our Company and part of the 1st Bramford. I well remember helping to make our first roly-poly pudding for lunch, when we used more suet than flour and every scrap of it was eaten. There was an everlasting trek for water and wood, so quickly used up, but our camp-fires were wonderful. Our tins of dried orange-peel, collected through the year, started the most obstinate of fires; I can smell the scent of peel and pine to this day!

We had good equipment, and replaced any that was needed from our funds, which every girl helped to swell. There was no shortage of fund-raising ideas— although we didn't go on sponsored walks or swims in those days!

When I was fifteen, we went again to this same beauty-spot, but at sixteen Kay and I left this part of the country and we became Lone Guides. Our letter-page was passed around to others in the same plight, each Guide adding news of interest, and ideas, but after a while this fizzled out. We never lost interest in the Guide Movement, though, and how wonderful it is to know that Guiding still goes on — different but the same as ever!

CATCH ME A WOODPECKER

by LEIGHTON HOUGHTON

"Have you heard what Gipsy's planning for Saturday week?" Angela spoke breathlessly, trotting behind Elizabeth, trying to keep up with her. "Another Tramp Supper—like last year—on the waste ground behind the school."

"Not again?" Elizabeth stopped and regarded Angela with a look of disgust. "That's stale—honestly!"

Angela said, rather doubtfully, "Last year it was quite a success. Well, I mean, practically everybody dressed up, and it is something different."

"Last year we were kids," said Elizabeth. "This year we're not—or, at least, I'm not. Doesn't Gipsy realise that people grow up? I mean, everybody coming in tatty old clothes and frying sausages—and only girls!"

"It's meant to be a sort of Company party," said Angela, "just for the Guides."

"At least she might think of asking the Scouts to join us. Now, there would be a bit of fun in that—but just girls!"

Elizabeth was nearly fifteen, and she had confessed to Angela on more than one occasion that she was growing tired of Guides; she imagined that she was too old for Guides now; she wanted something different, and there was no Ranger unit in the district.

"I told Gipsy she ought to ask the Scouts to join in," said Angela, "but most of them are helping to run the dance at the Town Hall in aid of the Old People's Christmas Fund."

"Then she ought to change the day," declared Elizabeth. "I don't fancy just girls."

"You don't have to come," said Angela, beginning to feel rather cross at Elizabeth's attitude.

"Oh, don't I! Gipsy is thick with my mum and I'd need a cast-iron excuse to wriggle out of it. Don't forget I'm P.L. of the Woodpeckers. That's the worst of being a P.L.; you always have to be at whatever's going on. I think I shall give up Guides and join the Youth Club, but I'm not going

to till I've got my Stalker badge to complete my Woodcraft emblem. If she's putting on her stupid Tramp Supper I shall have to turn up, but I shan't enjoy it."

They walked on in silence, climbing the steep road which led out of the houses towards the open country, Elizabeth swinging her camera by its strap and humming to herself.

It was her determination to gain the Stalker badge that had brought her out on this rather chilly spring morning. For a week or two she had worked for the Stalker badge. She had spent patient hours in the copse on the hill above Brandwood Farm and had succeeded in taking three photographs of wild birds there. She had got two very sharp pictures of a hedgesparrow and a chaffinch and a rather indistinct one of a jay, which had flown off just as she clicked the shutter, screeching its warning to other birds.

The 1st Brandwood Guide Company had been formed on a new estate close on five years ago. Elizabeth had been one of the first members. Angela was in the same Patrol—the Woodpeckers. Though there were plenty of young people on the estate, it had been a struggle to keep the Company alive. Only by constantly arranging special meetings had Gipsy, the Guide Guider, managed to keep up

reached the gate of a sloping field that rose towards a knot of trees on the horizon. "I've heard them drumming and I spotted one of their nesting-places weeks ago, but they're so shy; they never come near enough for a picture."

"Wait for me!" Angela scrambled hastily on to the top bar of the gate, throwing a nervous glance towards a herd of bullocks between them and the copse. "Wait a minute, Liz!"

"You're not scared, are you?" Elizabeth paused. "They're only bullocks; they wouldn't hurt a fly."

The bullocks stopped grazing and stood in a solid huddle, gazing at the two girls. Elizabeth

"Shoo, you silly things!" Elizabeth called. "Make way! Shoo!"

the girls' interest. Last year a Tramp Supper had proved one of her most successful ideas.

The 1st Brandwood Scout Troop, formed at the same time, but meeting now in their own HQ., had met similar difficulties to those of the Guides; but their troubles had been partly overcome by the building of their own headquarters. The Guides, who had never succeeded in arousing the same enthusiasm among parents as the Scouts, still met in the school hall. On one or two occasions attempts had been made to bring Scouts and Guides together in a joint activity, but somehow support had always been lacking.

"If only I can snap a woodpecker." Elizabeth

marched forward boldly, swinging the camera. Two of the bullocks suddenly dipped their heads, bucked and trotted to one side. Angela gave a little cry of fear.

"All you've got to do is to go on walking," said Elizabeth, slackening her pace. "They'll make way."

The bullocks, however, did not make way. They stood solidly in front of the girls, barring their path.

"Can't we go round the next field?" asked Angela nervously.

"I suppose we could," replied Elizabeth doubtfully. She had stopped. "Shoo, you silly things! Make way! Shoo!"

The bullocks remained unimpressed. They stared at the girls—in a very hostile way, Angela thought nervously! The nearest one was only two or three yards away, and Elizabeth dared not advance any further. With a sigh of annoyance, she turned round. Then she saw that other bullocks had moved behind them and were barring their way back, standing between them and the gate. The only escape appeared to be by way of the hedge, which was thick and thorny.

"Oh, dear!" said Angela, her voice trembling. "I wish I hadn't come."

"I'm sure they wouldn't hurt us," said Elizabeth, not very convincingly. "Let's try to—"

She was interrupted by a shrill whistle from the direction of the gate. A Scout in uniform was leaning against it, straddling a bicycle. He grinned at them.

"Having trouble?"

"Well," said Elizabeth, hating to admit her defeat, "we do want to get past these bullocks, but—"

"Hold on!" The Scout dismounted, vaulted the gate, paused to pull a stick out of the hedge and advanced, waving it. "Get along, there! Scram! Hey up, hey up!"

The bullocks backed away from him. One of

As Elizabeth raised the camera, a crash came

them spun round and seemed to be charging at the two girls. Angela uttered a stifled scream and clutched Elizabeth's arm. The bullock changed its mind and swung away. The Scout, waving his stick and shouting, drove the animals towards the far end of the field. He came back to the two Guides, grinning.

"You'll be all right now. Can't think why girls are scared of cows. Where were you going, anyway?"

"To the copse." Elizabeth felt annoyed; she would much rather have driven the bullocks off by herself. "Thank you for helping us."

"Not at all. Bullocks are pretty harmless," said the Scout, making no move to leave. "You're 1st Brandwood Guides, aren't you?"

"Yes," said Elizabeth.

"I'm 1st Brandwood, too. Saturday-week we're staging a dance at the Town Hall; it's going to be great. Are you coming?"

"No," said Elizabeth. "We've got a do of our own—a Tramp Supper. Come on, Angy; let's go."

The Scout remained standing in the field. He watched them climb towards the trees.

"That was lucky," said Angela. "Nice, wasn't he?"

"Was he?" said Elizabeth. "I didn't notice."

She led the way to the woodpeckers' tree. There was a small hole in the trunk and the bark was stained with bird-lime. She selected a place some yards away and squatted down, screened by a bush, her camera trained on the hole. Angela crouched beside her. From the far side of the wood came the intermittent drumming of the birds.

"Ouch!" said Angela after several minutes. "I think I'm going to get cramp."

"Ssh!" Elizabeth frowned at her. "Keep still, or I'll never get a picture. There's one of them drumming quite near now."

"Maybe it isn't a nest," said Angela, after another lengthy pause. "Perhaps it's just a hole."

"Ssh!" said Elizabeth again.

There was a sudden harsh cry, a flash of colour, and a red-crested bird seemed to drop out of the overhanging foliage. For a fleeting second it clung to the trunk, its back towards them. Elizabeth drew in a sharp breath of excitement, raised her camera, and felt for the button. At the same instant a loud crashing sounded in the scrub behind them. The bird vanished.

"Bother!" Elizabeth lowered the camera. "That would have been a smashing picture. Botheration!"

"Oh, it's you!" The Scout was standing in the undergrowth, grinning at them. "Are you playing a game or something?"

"Oh, it's you!" The Scout grinned at them. "Are you playing a game or something?"

"No, we're not." Elizabeth felt furious. She stood up, not looking at him.

"I'm wooding." The information was received in silence. "I'm camping for the weekend—just for fun." There was another awkward pause. "I'm cooking breakfast—a bit late in the day. Would you care for a sausage?"

"No, thank you," said Elizabeth in what was intended to be an icy tone.

There was another long pause.

"Well, I'll be moving on." The Scout hesitated, but receiving no encouragement to stay turned and strolled away, whistling.

"Of all the idiots!" Elizabeth stamped her foot. "To burst in on us just at that minute! He ruined everything—just as I had a really super subject!"

"I wouldn't say no to a sausage," said Angela, in a small voice.

"He can keep his sausages!"

Elizabeth's father was a keen photographer. One of the upstairs rooms of his house was fitted out as a darkroom. It was he who originally suggested that Elizabeth should try to photograph birds for the Stalker badge. Now he followed this up by showing her how to set up trip-cotton for a flashlight photograph at night. Elizabeth was quite

excited by the idea of completing her photographs with a flashlight one of the elusive woodpecker.

She called for Angela after tea the same day, and they went back to the copse as dusk was settling over the countryside. Angela was relieved to find that there were no bullocks in the field. Beyond the trees to one side there was a faint glow of red.

"I think it's a fire," said Angela.

"It's that Scout!" Elizabeth quickened her pace. "I suppose that's where he's camping. For goodness' sake, don't let him spot us."

The fixing of the camera was a long and delicate operation. Elizabeth propped the camera firmly in the crotch of a tree, the lens trained on to the woodpecker's hole; she then fastened a fine, strong thread attached to the shutter-lever to the lip of the hole.

"The woodpecker can't possibly help knocking against it," Elizabeth explained; "then it will flash the bulb and click! The photo will be in the bag!"

"You hope!" said Angela doubtfully. "Won't the flash frighten the bird away?"

"Of course it will," retorted Elizabeth impatiently, "but by then the photo will be taken; it won't matter."

"Oh!" Angela was not entirely convinced. "What

do we do now? It's going to be pretty chilly waiting here and not moving."

"We don't have to wait, silly. We go away and leave it, and tomorrow we come back and find it all done. I'll only have to take the camera home and develop the film."

"Suppose it rains—won't it damage your camera?"

"It won't rain."

They had emerged from the trees and were crossing the field when a figure loomed up in front of them, approaching from the gate.

"Oh, hello! You two back again?"

It was the Scout. Angela stopped, but Elizabeth nudged her, moving on.

"Hello!" said Angela.

"I say, you wouldn't like to have a dekko at my camp, would you? I'll make you a cup of char."

"Sorry!" Elizabeth pushed past him. "We can't stop."

"I do think you might have," said Angela, as they climbed the gate.

"Might have *what*?" asked Elizabeth.

"Accepted his cup of tea. I think he's rather nice."

"Well, I don't. You can go back if you want to."

"He wasn't asking me," Angela answered. "Well, you know what I mean. It wasn't me he meant. He was asking you."

"Oh, hooey!" said Elizabeth, and was glad that the dusk hid her rising blush.

"Of course he was! I think you ought to have accepted. He wanted you to."

"Hooey!" said Elizabeth again and jumped from the gate. "Do hurry! You can call round tomorrow, if you like; I'll have the film developed by dinnertime. I can't wait to see it."

But when Angela called at the house next day she found Elizabeth in a bad temper.

"Didn't it work? I say, I am sorry!"

"Oh, it worked all right." Elizabeth closed the door and leant against it. "It was a marvellous photograph—I don't think. Do you want to see it?"

"Yes, please. Where is it?"

"Here!" Elizabeth held out a half-plate print. "Dad developed it for me and made an enlargement."

Angela took the picture and burst into suppressed giggles. There was a clear photograph of the tree and the woodpecker's hole, but framing them, on either side, were a pair of legs topped by shorts.

"What is it—who is it? Oh, I bet it's that Scout!" Angela could hardly speak for laughing. "He's wearing shorts for camping. He must have walked into your thread and flashed the camera."

"Of all the clumsy idiots, that Scout takes the prize. Of course it's the Scout. Who else could it be?"

Elizabeth snatched the picture back and tore it across. "Now I'll have to set the flash all over again!"

They went back to the copse that evening. The Scout was still there. He was wearing uniform now. He came to meet them as they crossed the field. Angela felt certain he had been watching for them.

"Hello!" He stood in their path, grinning.

"Hello!" said Elizabeth, not stopping.

"I say, I am sorry. I set off your flash, didn't I?"

"It doesn't matter." Elizabeth made to pass him, but he stepped in her way.

"I didn't realise it was there."

"Of course you didn't. I'm going to set it again now."

"I'll watch for it next time. What are you after —bird photographs?"

"Elizabeth's taken some smashing ones," Angela put in. "She's working for the Stalker badge."

"If I don't get another flash set up pretty soon it'll be too dark to do it."

"Sorry." The Scout stood to one side. "Can I help?"

"No, thank you," said Elizabeth, and hurried on.

The Scout was waiting for them when they came back.

"I say, I've just made coffee—" he began, but Elizabeth interrupted him.

"Mustn't stop," she said. "Angela's got to get home."

"Oh, I haven't!" said Angela indignantly.

"Well, I have. 'Bye!"

She walked quickly to the gate; Angela had to hurry to keep up with her.

"Honestly, I do think you're rude. He only wanted to be friendly. Besides, he likes you."

"Oh, shut up, Angy! He ruined my picture."

"If he'd ruined mine," said Angela wistfully, "I wouldn't have minded."

"You're soppy. If he goes near that tree tonight and sets off the flash I'll get really mad with him."

"You ought to have had his coffee."

"I hate coffee."

"So do I, but we needn't have drunk it."

"You're crackers," said Elizabeth.

She collected the camera very early next morning. There was no sign of the Scout.

"This time I'm developing it myself," she told Angela. "I'm not having all the family laughing at me again."

"Perhaps it didn't go off," said Angela pessimistically.

Angela shouted with laughter, while Elizabeth gazed furiously at the picture

"The thread was broken. Bet you I've got a beauty. You can come and watch me develop it, if you like."

Angela sat on a stool in the darkroom, which was illuminated by a red bulb. Elizabeth worked on the film. She was washing the exposed negative under the tap when she gave an exclamation.

"Not legs again?" said Angela, and peered over her shoulder.

Elizabeth didn't answer.

The negative was very small. It was impossible to make out detail, but it didn't appear to contain the picture of a woodpecker. The tree was there, and something white below the hole, clinging to the trunk.

"Whatever is it?" Angela peered at the negative, frowning. "Is it or isn't it a woodpecker?"

"It's the wrong shape for a woodpecker," said Elizabeth crossly. "There's something there, but I don't know what. As soon as it's dry I'll put it in the enlarger."

It was some while before the negative could be enlarged. When at last the moment arrived, Angela gazed eagerly at the white sheet on which Elizabeth was carefully focusing the picture. Suddenly it leaped into perspective—the trunk with its rough bark, the dark hole, the splashes of bird-lime . . .

"It's a piece of paper," said Angela.

There was a large sheet of paper tied on to the trunk with string, and there was writing on the paper—neatly lettered capitals which stood out boldly.

BLOW WOODPECKERS. I'VE GOT TWO TICKETS FOR THE DANCE ON SATURDAY. PLEASE WILL YOU COME?

"Well, of all the cheek!"

Angela collapsed on to the floor, where she shook with laugher.

Elizabeth gazed at her furiously, until slowly her expression relaxed and a smile began to crinkle round her mouth. "Isn't he the limit?" she said. "He says 'Blow woodpeckers'. We ought to have told him that we're Woodpeckers too!"

Two days later Angela found a note in her letterbox.

"*Please tell Gipsy that I can't make the Tramp Supper. I've got a date.—Liz.*"

Angela gazed at it a trifle wistfully. "Well, we couldn't both miss the Tramp Supper," she murmured.

CONTRIBUTIONS

Contributions to the *Girl Guide Annual* are welcomed throughout the year. Send with stamped and fully addressed *envelope* to: The Editor, Scouting/Guiding Annuals, Purnell & Sons Ltd., 49/50 Poland Street, London, W.1.

GLAD AND GAY

the Giddy Guides

by Eileen Chivers

Gabrielle and Gladys say,
"Our friends all call us Glad and Gay."

PANCAKE DAY

One week the Guides are all delighted
To hear that they have been invited
To attend a course of demonstrations
For those with cooking aspirations.

Glad and Gay both go along,
Resolved that nothing shall go wrong
They watch the demonstrator bake
A lovely date-and-walnut cake.

Each week they're shown some tempting dish
Of meat or pastry, fruit or fish.
And nothing happens to Glad and Gay
Until it comes to Pancake Day.

The Guides are told, "The way to **learn**
Is for you each to take a turn."
They toss the pancakes nearly all
And catch them neatly as they fall.

It's Glad's turn next. Her catch is poor;
The pancake lands upon the floor.
Her friend Gay whispers, "Don't be vexed.
Remember it is my turn next."

She flips the pancake in the air;
It falls to earth—they know not where.
Of all the pancakes that are tossed
Gay's is the only one that's lost.

The Guides are saying their goodbyes.
"Why, there's the pancake!" someone cries.
"It's on a peg! Well, fancy that!
It looks exactly like a hat!"

Don't Get Tied Up In Knots

says F. Travis

If you can tie a Reef Knot you can almost tie a Grocer's Knot and a Surgeon's Knot. These two knots are very much like the Reef Knot, and as simply tied, but all three are really different knots with different uses, and so they have different names.

REEF KNOT. This is for joining ropes, etc., of the same thickness, and is used in first-aid because it lies flat and so does not hurt the patient. The GROCER'S KNOT is a Reef Knot with an extra twist in the first part of it. It is useful for tying

holds while the knot is finished off, and so does not need anyone's finger on it to prevent it from slipping. The SURGEON'S KNOT is a Reef Knot finished off with an extra twist. It is used where an ordinary Reef Knot would not hold because of slippery ends, or for some similar reason.

SHEET BEND. This is for joining ropes of unequal thickness. The thinner rope is

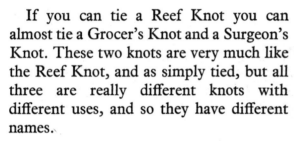

up the neck of a kitbag or sack, or for a bundle or parcel so long as the knot is against something firm. The extra twist

entwined round a bight (loop) of the thicker one, with the ends coming out on the same side. The DOUBLE SHEET

BEND is an ordinary (or single) Sheet Bend with the entwining turn followed by an extra one lying flat beside it. It is used when a single Sheet Bend will not hold, either because the ropes are slippery or because one is much thicker than the other.

then finished off by continuing in the same direction and passing the running end under the second turn. The MAGNUS HITCH is a Clove Hitch with an extra turn in the middle. You tie a Clove Hitch, leaving enough running end

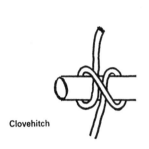

Clovehitch

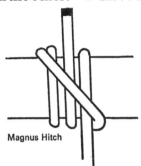

Magnus Hitch

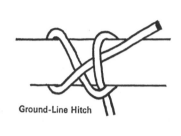

Ground-Line Hitch

The BINDER TURN is started like a single Sheet Bend, but instead of finishing off by passing the entwining end under itself it is passed over itself, then back under itself, finishing up as a thumb-knot round the bight of the other rope. The thumb-knot should be pulled tight to prevent the bight opening out, and so making sure that the two ends point the same way, which is the special feature of this knot. It is used for attaching to a rope that has to be pulled through machinery, a pulley block, or any small space where a rope end would get in the way.

CLOVE HITCH. This is for securing a rope to a spar or post or anything similar. It is tied by making two turns round the spar with the running end, but the first turn crosses over itself at the start of the second turn so that the running end will come round on the other side of the standing part. The knot is

for an extra turn. Bring the end round in the same direction as the other turns, and pass it through between them. This knot, often used by builders, has a tighter grip than the Clove Hitch, especially on smooth spars. The GROUND-LINE HITCH has two turns, like the Clove Hitch, but instead of the running end finishing off by going under the second turn it goes over it and under the first turn. This knot will stand movement in any direction without working loose.

ROUND TURN AND TWO HALF-HITCHES. This is for making fast a rope under strain, such as securing a rope in strong wind, or tethering a self-willed animal. The round turn takes the strain while the half-hitches are tied. The knot is simply a full turn of the rope round a spar or post, then two half-hitches (a Clove Hitch) tied round the standing part of the rope. The HALF TURN

Round Turn

and

Two Half-Hitches

Half-Turn

and

Two Half-Hitches

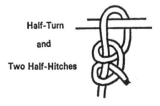

Fisherman's Bend

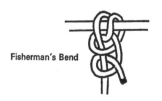

AND TWO HALF-HITCHES (sometimes called simply Two Half-Hitches) has a half turn round the spar instead of a full turn because it is used when there is no strain on the rope. The FISHERMAN'S as when secured to the handle of a water bucket down a well or over a ship's side, or when attached to an anchor ring.

BOWLINE. This is a loop that will not slip, and is made in the end of a rope.

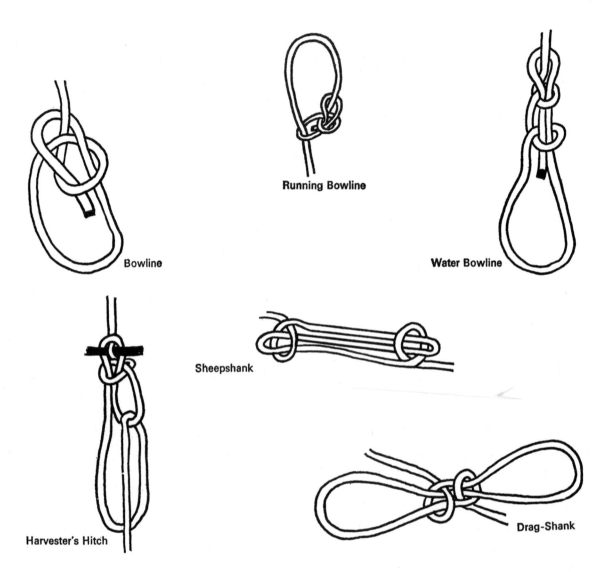

Running Bowline

Bowline

Water Bowline

Sheepshank

Harvester's Hitch

Drag-Shank

BEND (also known as the Fisherman's Hitch, the Bucket Hitch, and the Anchor Bend, and very different from the Fisherman's Knot) is the same as the Round Turn and Two Half-Hitches, except that the first half-hitch is taken through the round turn. This prevents the knot jamming under strain, especially when wet, It is made by passing the running end through a small loop in the standing part, taking the end round the standing part, then back down through the small loop. The RUNNING BOWLINE is a running noose, and can be used as a lariat. Start by making a small Bowline. It need not be much bigger than your fist. Then put your hand through it, grasp the standing part and pull it through. The WATER BOWLINE is a Bowline with a half-hitch in the loop. This bears most of the strain and prevents the knot from jamming, especially when wet. To tie it, start to make an ordinary Bowline, but after taking the end up through the small loop (or half-hitch), go on to make another small loop a little way farther along the standing part, and finish off through that. The half-hitch should be worked

Slip Reef

Hitch, then take the rest of the rope round the axle and up through the loop of the Harvester's Hitch. Pull the load down tight, and make the rope fast to the axle with a Clove Hitch or other suitable knot. The DRAG-SHANK is a middle-

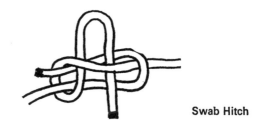

Swab Hitch

up to within an inch or so of the finished knot, and the running end should be passed through it.

SHEEPSHANK. This is for shortening a rope, or for taking the strain off the weak part in a rope. It is made by gathering up the slack into two parallel bights and securing the end of each in a half-hitch. The HARVESTER'S HITCH (or Rope Tackle) is a Sheepshank with only one end half-hitched, leaving a loop at the other end. The short loop at the half-hitched end should be toggled with the standing part, or seized to it with twine, or a half-hitch round the standing part can be made with the short loop itself. This knot is used by farmers, lorry-drivers, and others transporting loads. To secure a load of wood on a trek-cart, for example, first (before making the Harvester's Hitch) fasten an end to the axle and throw the rope over the load to the other side. On that side, two or three feet above axle level, make the Harvester's

man knot. It is a means of making a loop in a rope without using the ends. For instance, to make a hand-grip loop in the middle of a rope, for helping to drag a log or pull a trek-cart, make a Sheepshank about a foot long, slide the half-hitches to the centre and bring the resulting two loops together to form the grip. The Sheepshank can, if required, be made big enough for the loops to go over one shoulder, or both. The loops are easily adjustable to equal size.

To turn a Reef Knot into a SLIP REEF make a half bow of it; finish it off with one end doubled. If you do the same when finishing off a Sheet Bend, you will have tied a SWAB HITCH. Both these are used when only a temporary knot is needed, or for quick release. The Slip Reef is used in camp for tying brailing tapes.

Some of the knots here are shown open to make them easier to follow. They should be finished off tight.

Fun with Wood

by Erica Meijer

In this very interesting article, a Dutch expert gives you practical guidance on the fascinating handcraft of whittling, which offers a satisfying outlet for artistic and creative hands.

Your pocket-knife has many uses—but apart from its usefulness on practical occasions it is an excellent instrument for a kind of handcraft which gives pleasure and satisfaction, a handcraft which can hardly be called expensive and which can be fascinating in its wide and varying possibilities. It can be done at any time of the year and has only one drawback: you will make a mess wherever you practise it!

And now the unbelievable: Anybody can do it! That is a challenge, I know, but you try and see.

We are talking about whittling.

Now what do you need?

A strong and really sharp knife.

A small hacksaw, like the ones you often use in camp.

A bit of wood suitable for whatever you decide to make.

Immediately you will ask: What is a suitable bit of wood?

Well, first of all, don't try to use either too soft or too hard a kind of wood. With the soft kind, you will find that your knife cuts away disastrous quantities rather suddenly, and with the hard kind you need a degree of skill which takes time to acquire.

Suitable kinds of wood for whittling are: Lime, birch, rowan, horsechestnut.

These are nice and easy to work with, yet tough enough not to break while you work.

Of the harder kinds you may want to use in future, try: Cherry, apple, pear, whitebeam.

These kinds take on a very warm reddish colour.

Now, where do you find this wood? For our purpose, take a walk in your garden, go out in the country, or, best of all, look around while you are in camp.

It is absolutely essential to start on an easy thing which can be made out of one piece of wood, and for which your Guide knife is suitable.

There are several things you can make which look very attractive and effective, and which do not call for a lot of work or skill. All you have to do is to cut patterns in the *bark* of the wood—patterns like your Patrol emblem, or just fancy ones, which give life and decorative charm to any object you want to make. You can either cut away the pattern you have drawn in the bark, or leave the pattern and cut away the surrounding bark.

The simplest way to get an effect is by cutting away strips of bark to make a design, and then colouring the design with poster paint. It is best to varnish it afterwards to make it weatherproof and bring out the colours (diagram I).

Having made a few experiments, you will want to start really cutting into the wood and shaping a real object. What

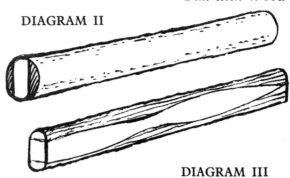

DIAGRAM II

DIAGRAM III

about making a paperknife or a butter knife?

Be careful not to cut away too much! You can never put it back, you see.

Start by making your piece of wood flat on both sides (diagram II), then draw the outlines on it and cut away the bits you don't need any longer (diagram III). Now work the object gradually all over so that you get the desired shape and thickness. Don't work on one part only, or you may discover that you have gone crooked and have cut away rather too much to get the whole thing straight again.

The moment will come when you decide you have cut away just enough, and what you have made looks quite like a paperknife except for being rather bumpy. That is the time to use sandpaper—not too smooth a kind—and rub until your paperknife is smooth all over. Then take the finest sandpaper you can get, and finish off with this. To your delight, you will discover that a shine appears as if the thing was polished, and the longer you keep on sandpapering the better polish you will get.

It is always a good thing when making an object to bear in mind the uses to which it will be put. The most attractive things are usually those which serve their purpose best. Think for instance of your

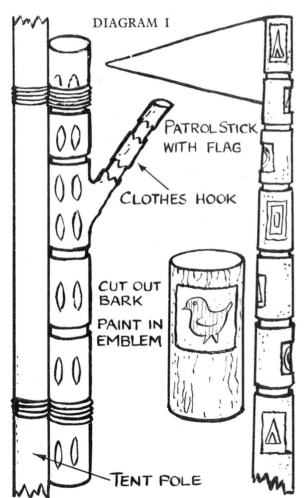

DIAGRAM I

PATROL STICK WITH FLAG

CLOTHES HOOK

CUT OUT BARK

PAINT IN EMBLEM

TENT POLE

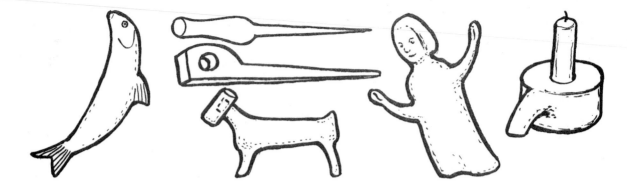

paperknife. It is meant to open letters. So it must not be too clumsy or thick. It needs a handle to hold on to, and also a sharp point which can enter an envelope. It has to be sharp-edged so that it really *cuts* a letter open and doesn't tear it; otherwise you might as well tear with your fingers.

Some attractive objects to whittle are illustrated in the *Guide Handbook*.

Now here are a few points to remember:

1. Use green rather than dead wood, but not too green, as then it will probably warp and burst after a few days. Dead wood is brittle and breaks, besides being bad for the knife.

2. Be sure your knife is really *sharp*. Keep it sharpened. Use a carborundum and not the doorstep or wall of your house.

3. Choose pieces of wood without knots, as these are treacherous and extremely hard.

4. Don't cut branches and twigs thoughtlessly wherever you happen to spot them.

5. Always try to cut *with* the grain. It is easier.

6. Please remember: Always cut *away* from the hand which is holding the wood. Then if your knife shoots out

of control it will not cut your fingers. This is important, as your knife is very sharp.

We have kept the best and most fascinating part of whittling till the end. It does not require a great deal of skill, but does ask quite a lot of your powers of observation and imagination.

No doubt you have all seen funny and quite realistic shapes in clouds and outlines of trees now and then? Well, this is what we are going to do.

Any time you are outside on a walk in the country, on a hike, or in camp, you will probably see dead branches, twigs, bits of tree-roots, or chips left by wood-cutters.

Now try combining your observation power with your imagination. Pick up a queerly shaped piece of wood, hold it several ways up, and perhaps you will suddenly discover the outline of an animal which with a little help from your knife (perhaps cutting away bits or glueing in bits) can be made to look like a real animal. You will understand what is meant if you study the illustration above.

This kind of whittling is really the most thrilling. It's fun to try to "see things" in wood, and to be able to shape something nice and useful out of it. It adds interest to your hikes and walks anywhere in the country, and the faculty for "visualising" grows with practice.

Now a last word of warning. Please don't attempt the impossible with an unsuitable piece of wood or the wrong kind of knife. For instance, don't try to make a spoon. You will never be able to hollow out the right shape with an ordinary knife. If you feel you simply must make spoons you will have to get a specially shaped gouge that will do the job.

Well, it is time to gather together your Patrol. Perhaps you may not all want to start whittling, but what about setting out on a "hunt-for-shapes-in-wood"? Challenge another Patrol, and see who can make the most original and varied exhibition of the finds. You will be surprised how interesting and exciting this kind of "hunt" can be.

PICK THE FLOWERS

by Jean Franklin

Find the names of six flowers suggested by the six rhymes. Write down their names, then from the first letter of each one spell out the name of another flower.

1. The beast and what his jaws might do
   To the garden flower will give a clue.

2. Did the saint who number one did slay
   Need zeal plus two to kill his prey?

3. A part of the ear plus three letters might
   Make the border look a pretty sight.

4. The pretty garden-flower brings
   To mind an instrument with strings.

5. Name the rainbow goddess who could be said
   To be in the eye and the flower-bed.

6. A vegetable to bring tears—surely not,
   But a dweller in the flower plot.

RIDDLE-ME-REE

by Helen N. Martindale

My first is in cold but not in hot,
My second's in lamp but not in torch,
My third is in mop but not in top,
My fourth is in pan but not in scorch,
My whole is somewhere you may have been—
Guides always go there when they're really keen.

ANSWER: CAMP

Which Wood For

Holly logs will burn like wax—
You should burn them green.
Elm logs like smouldering flax—
No flame to be seen.

Pear logs and apple logs,
They will scent your room.
Cherry logs across the dogs
Smell like flowers in bloom.

But ash logs all smooth and grey,
Burn them green or old;
Buy up all that come your way—
They're worth their weight in gold.

Your Camp Fire?

Oak logs will warm you well
If they're old and dry;
Larch logs of pine woods smell;
But the sparks will fly.

Beech logs for Christmas time;
Yew logs heat well.
"Scotch" logs it is a crime
For anyone to sell.

Birch logs will burn too fast,
Chestnut scarce at all;
Hawthorn logs are good to last
If cut in the fall.

How many trees can you name?

Gracious Guiding

by Hilary Burgess

"Such a pity that good manners are out of date!" We've all heard the older generation saying that, haven't we? Well, it just isn't true. Often we just don't think, and often it's shyness, not bad manners, that makes us fall a little short in our observance of the Guide Law "A Guide is polite and considerate". Don't you agree? Sometimes we don't know quite the right thing to do or say—and so do or say nothing rather than the wrong thing.

Do you find it difficult to introduce strangers to each other—knowing just the right thing to say? It's not easy, is it? Here is a tip or two. You always introduce the man to the woman. "Mrs. Brown, may I introduce Mr. Smith?" And a single woman to a married woman —"Miss Green, I would like to introduce you to Mrs. Pink." And if you happen to be introduced to anyone try to think of anything to say rather than "Pleased to meet you", which somehow is just not quite right! "I am so glad; I've heard a lot about you", or "I've wanted to know you for such a long time". Practise phrases in the bath when you know you are going to a party and are sure to be introduced to new people—grown-ups, I mean.

At school today you are sometimes told not to stand up when the Headmistress comes into the classroom. It's understand-able when in the middle of a lesson, but at any other time it is gracious to get up the minute an older person comes into the room. I've so often seen a Commissioner visit a Guide meeting when all that happens is a rather awed stare from the Guides. Not a very friendly welcome, is it?—and remember she is probably just as nervous at being faced with all of you as you are at her visit! A Guidy welcome makes all the difference to her and her feelings.

Being gracious is really the art of putting yourself in the position of the other person. How would you feel if you went, possibly as a stranger, to visit a collection of people, and all you received was a vacant stare?

If it so happens that your Commissioner has a title—her name might be Lady Snips—don't be afraid of saying, "How do you do, Lady Snips—will you come and look at our Patrol home?" And if you aren't sure how to address her, she will never mind being asked so that you can introduce your Patrol. And remember you introduce them to her—"Lady Snips, this is Mary Brown."

Perhaps this Christmas you will have a dinner party at home, and you will be needed to help. Here's a tip for you: if you are taking round the dish of potatoes, etc., you stand behind the guest's left shoulder so she can use her right hand to take her helping. When you clear the plates you take from the right-hand side of the person at the table.

Think for a moment of the most gracious woman you know, someone who is able to put others at ease at once, someone who is easy to talk to and able to fit into any situation she finds herself in—a camp, a jumble sale, a dinner party—she always has the right word for the occasion; she is able to talk to Granny as easily as she is able to play with the small baby brother, and equally make the right remark to the sophisticated 18-year-old.

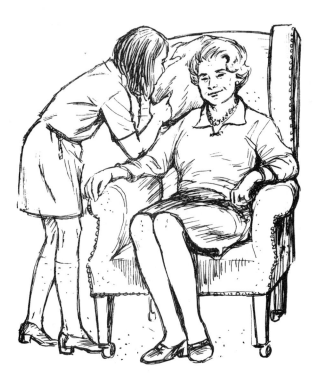

It's a wonderful gift—and not very many people have it. It's not always a thing that comes naturally; but you will find that people who have it are unselfish and considerate for others' feelings. They never put themselves and their wants first, and so as they grow up and mature so does this great gift of graciousness. I'm sure you will know such a woman. Watch her, and learn from her.

How hard some of us find it to say "Thank you" graciously! Adults think round the gift they are going to give you for your birthday or for Christmas; they choose with care the very article they hope will give pleasure—and sometimes it's weeks before that "thank you" letter is written. If the present is given in person, they are shattered by just a "Thanks", and that's all. It may be a pair of gloves they've taken hours to knit, so do remember that it costs nothing to be gracious and grateful, and means so much. Another small tip—wear those gloves the next time you go to tea with Aunty: she will be so pleased, even if they were not just the colour that you wanted!

Home is the place we really love most, and think about the least. Mum works hard and loves every member of her family, but how seldom does she have a word of appreciation or gratitude! Just remember to give her that comfy chair when she sits down at the end of a day. Say, "Supper was lovely, Mum—my favourite today", and she will feel a warm glow inside!

When in doubt on a point of good manners or etiquette ask and find out. Be natural and be sincere and you won't go wrong. Don't mind being told, and, once more, never be afraid to ask.

In Guiding we try to be courteous, thoughtful, and considerate.

NIGHT ALARM

AN EXCITING GUIDE CAMP ADVENTURE IN PICTURES

Adapted by Robert Moss

STOP, STOP! D'YOU HEAR ME, SULTAN? WHOA!

GOT YOU! I COULDN'T HAVE HELD ON MUCH LONGER. THANK GOODNESS YOU GAVE IN FIRST!

IT'S HILARY. WHAT IN THE WORLD IS SHE DOING OUT WITH A HORSE AT THIS TIME OF NIGHT?

IT'S BARBARA PREECE'S PONY. IT WAS PROWLING ROUND OUR TENT, AND HILARY WENT OUT TO CATCH IT!

HILARY'S GOING TO BE A HORSE-BREAKER WHEN SHE GROWS UP!

NEXT MORNING THE GUIDER SENT A MESSAGE TO BARBARA PREECE THAT HER PONY HAD BEEN CAUGHT AND WAS AT THE CAMP

WE WERE ALL WAKENED IN THE DEAD OF NIGHT. YOUR PONY WAS GALLOPING ROUND THE FIELD, WITH HILARY HANGING ON TO THE END OF HIS ROPE LIKE GRIM DEATH

I THINK EVEN YOU WOULD ADMIT THAT HILARY HAS COURAGE, BARBARA PREECE, IF YOU'D SEEN HOW SHE WAS CARRIED ROUND THE FIELD BY YOUR PONY

THERE'S YOUR PONY, BARBARA

BUT IT ISN'T — THAT'S THE JOKE! SULTAN WALKED BACK INTO HIS PADDOCK LAST EVENING. SULTAN IS A QUIET PONY. THE PONY YOU ROPED LAST NIGHT IS ONE OF THE WILD FOREST PONIES. I DON'T WONDER IT LED YOU A DANCE!

I TAKE BACK ALL I SAID! I WOULDN'T HAVE DARED HANG ON TO A WILD PONY AS YOU DID. YOU'RE JOLLY BRAVE.

IF I HEAR ANYTHING ELSE OUTSIDE OUR TENT I'LL TAKE CARE NOT TO WAKE HILARY!

I'LL UNTIE YOU AND LET YOU GO NOW, OLD BOY. HERE'S AN APPLE BY WAY OF AN APOLOGY FOR GIVING YOU SUCH A DISTURBED NIGHT!

IF PONIES DREAM THAT WILD ONE OUGHT TO HAVE NIGHTMARES FOR A WEEK ABOUT OUR HILARY ROPING IT!

WELL, WE'VE CERTAINLY GOT SOMETHING TO PUT IN OUR CAMP LOG-BOOK!

THE END

CAMP REFRIGERATOR

Trevor Holloway Shows You How to Make It

BOWL OF WATER   STRIPS OF CLOTH

SACKING

Every Guide knows the difficulty of keeping perishable foods fresh when camping during warm weather. Butter turns to an oily mess, milk goes "off", bread becomes as dry as sawdust, and so forth.

Obviously you can't transport a domestic "fridge" to your camp site, but you *can* contrive a very efficient makeshift. The home-made job seen in the illustration won't enable you to make ice-cream or deep-freeze your precious perishables, but it will keep them at a temperature considerably below that of a warm summer's day, which is the chief thing.

The "fridge" works on the principle of heat insulation, and the inside temperature of the box is kept down by water-cooling.

First, you will need a wooden box, which should be draped over the top and around the sides with sacking or similar material.

A large-sized bowl, or a bucket, should be filled with water and placed on top of the box. Several strips of absorbent material about two inches wide must be placed with their ends in the reservoir of water and allowed to trail over the edges and down the sides of the sacking-covered box. As the strips become saturated, they conduct water into the material draping the box. This process of satura-

tion will be speeded up if the draping material is thoroughly damped beforehand.

Strangely enough, the warmer the day the cooler is the inside of the refrigerator. Actually, it is most effective when exposed to the sun.

Once made, all that is necessary is to top up the water supply occasionally. You can, if you wish, fit some legs and shelves to your model. Two support legs will do, but four are really better.

By the way, although the model described here has been suggested for camp use, something similar could be devised for home use during the summer months. In this case, of course, a shallow tray would be necessary below the refrigerator to catch the water which drips from the saturated material.

GUIDE ROBIN HOODS

Lone Pine Bowmen, who are Scouts of the 3rd Collier Row Group, Essex, instruct Guides of the 1st Collier Row Company in the first steps of archery

On target! Guides remove arrows very carefully to avoid damaging them

WORLD-WIDE GUIDING

When the Girl Scouts of South Korea held their first international Jamboree to commemorate sixty years of Guiding, they were visited by Mrs Park Chung Hee, the First Lady of the Republic, who is President of the Korean Girl Scouts and addressed the 700 campers who came to the Jamboree from nine countries

113

Girls in the Gang Show

by Valerie Peters

With photographs by Jack Olden and Harold Wyld

Guides and Rangers make an attractive chorus in the London Gang Show Photo: Handford Photography

The London Gang Show belonged solely to Scouting for many years. Now there are Ranger Guides and Guiders in the show, and the accent has changed from boys and men to boys and girls, which gives the show a more youthful quality. There are plenty of attractive girls in the Guide Movement, girls with the personality and enthusiasm the Gang Show requires.

The London Gang Show has been going since 1932 and has raised thousands of pounds for Scouting. Profit comes not only from the fortnight of performances each year, but from the scores of local Scout Gang Shows which make use of the London Show's songs and sketches. Behind the Show one man stands out as the master-mind, and that is Ralph Reader, its director, who started the Gang forty

114

Ralph Reader interviews members of the Guide Movement eager to appear in the Gang Show

years ago. A famous producer and choreographer, and a dedicated Scouter, he brought Scouting into the world of entertainment and found an ideal way of raising valuable funds for the Scout Movement. Today the Show is more popular than ever, with songs, dancing and sketches, and a team of boys and girls.

The Gang is one large family. Many of the cast have brothers and sisters appearing, and this helps to make the Show the really good family entertainment that it is.

What is it like to be a girl in the Gang?

Girls in the Gang are often trained dancers or singers, although not in the professional sense. They have had dancing lessons at some time and have a fair idea of the techniques involved in show dancing. At the auditions their main worry is their faces and their figures. The faces may be pretty, but the figures may call for dieting beforehand. Naturally, the producer is not looking just for a pretty face. The auditions are not too nerve-racking, and there is always a pleasant atmosphere. They are held at Baden-Powell House, London, during the spring. Groups of six are asked to run through some dance steps together. This is simply to see whether they have any feeling for rhythm and timing. After the initial group auditions, there is time for soloists to go on stage and do their party pieces. Then it is all over. Soon the lucky ones will receive letters requesting their attendance at rehearsals.

The rehearsals are also held at Baden-Powell House—every Tuesday and some Sundays. The girls in the Gang make many friends among the rest of the cast, who come from all over London and the home counties. Ralph Reader, like any other producer, believes in concentration and hard work, and there must be silence while rehearsals are in progress,

One of the Gang Show girls brings along a baby-sitter while she rehearses

as the girls soon find out. But he is also a kind and considerate producer, and effort does not go unnoticed.

The most important thing that the girls must remember is to keep in step and in time, and actually enjoy doing so. The dancing in a recent Gang Show was especially difficult. In a scene like *Moulin Rouge* the dance routine was a Gang version of the Can-Can. The rehearsal time goes all too quickly, and soon the girls are being fitted up for their costumes, and their photographs taken for their local papers.

In the weeks before the Show everyone gets rather nervous and apprehensive. In some of the numbers there are so many people on stage that it is difficult not to become confused. The idea is to concentrate on your own steps so that you

are not easily influenced by anyone else making a mistake. Most of the girls know that their families will be coming along to watch them and that their picture will appear in the local press; all this adds to the mounting anxiety.

The dress rehearsal arrives, a first performance for the cast in the actual theatre, the Odeon, Golder's Green, London. Here at last everything comes together—scenery, lighting, costumes, production—culminating in the final dress-rehearsal run-through in front of an invited audience. The Show opens on the following night.

The girls get to the theatre in plenty of time and step into their costumes. Any last-minute adjustments are quickly put right by the wardrobe team, and the girls join the make-up queue. The cast learn never to be surprised at what can happen in that queue. On one occasion before a Saturday matinee an old lady joined the make-up queue, having followed some Scouts into the theatre. Seeing them line up, she thought it was for a local Scout jumble sale!

Once made-up, the cast retire one by one to the dressing-rooms to wait for their calls. Someone comes in who has been out front and reports that the audience are starting to arrive and take their seats. Everyone imagines their family sitting in the auditorium, and nerves come creeping back. Legs feel like jelly and are certainly not capable of dancing!

Over the dressing-room speaker the cast marshal's voice calls for beginners, and the sound of hurrying feet on the staircase is heard. Those left in the communal girls' dressing-room are suddenly silent, listening for the orchestra to strike up the overture, and then the curtain is up. On to the stage tumble row after row of the Gang to the familiar strains of *We're Riding Along on the Crest of a Wave* and *Here We Are Again,* and to the welcoming applause of the already enthusiastic audience. Soon the girls themselves are running down the stairs in their grass skirts for their opening number, *Hawaii.*

Backstage during the Show is a real military operation. Girls and boys are coming and going—changing in and out of costumes—renovating or changing their make-up. Then, standing in the wings, they prepare to launch themselves on to the stage for yet another eye-catching spectacular.

All too soon it is the finale, and everyone is quite sad at having to say goodbye to such a marvellous audience. There will never be another night quite like the first night. A small Scout pulls Ralph Reader on to the stage to a burst of thunderous applause and plenty of curtain calls. It is over.

Backstage again, everyone crowds around congratulating each other, proud to be in the Gang. Ahead, there is a fortnight of performances, and each night will be better than the last. Then it will be over for the year—a sad thought. The girls put on their party frocks for the after-the-Show party.

During a recent Show the Gang fitted in rehearsals for a Gang Show Christmas Special, which they recorded for BBC1 with such famous stars as Peter Sellars, Dick Emery, Cardew Robinson and Reg Dixon. The girls showed up splendidly in their gay costumes and gave a wonderful display of dancing.

For the Gang audiences the Show is good family entertainment, but for the girls in the Gang it means quite a lot more. It is a chance to appear in a London Show, it is an opportunity to work with members of the Scout Movement, and it is a time to enjoy working in a team and to present to the public a small section of the Guide Movement in a new light—Girls in the Gang Show.

All on stage at the Gang Show

THE TWO-TREASURES HUNT

by C. CARTLIDGE

"I know what it is!" cried Mandy

"I don't like Linda, our new Guide, much," remarked Sue. "She's too superior."

"She doesn't seem very friendly," agreed Kate. "She may feel strange, though, and her standoffishness may be just a sort of defence."

"She's been a Guide before," little Mandy pointed out. "She's moved about a lot, I believe, and lived in lots of different towns."

"Well, the Swallows are welcome to her," said Sue.

Miss Page, the Guider, was holding up her hand for silence. "Now, Guides, to finish off the evening there's a special kind of treasure hunt I've arranged. It's quite short and simple, and I'm sure you'll all enjoy it." She handed each Patrol Leader a paper. "Here are the clues to follow. You should all be back here by dusk. Keep in your Patrols. Now off you go!"

The Robins gathered round their P.L., Kate, who read out what was written on the paper.

"Over stile, by meadow sweet,
  Past farm and house where three roads meet.
  Now just near here is quite a tease—
  Trace diamond necklace through the trees."

"We might have guessed our poetic Miss Page would turn out clues in verse!" laughed Sue.

"Wait a minute!" said Kate. "I haven't finished. There's some more." She continued:

  "On steep hill you may rest awhile;
  Then make your way down flowery aisle."

"There are several stiles near here," remarked Mandy, "but the one we want is by the meadow, so let's go."

"We'd better!" said Kate. "The Swallows are already on their way."

The Swallows, with their new Guide, Linda, in front with Helen, the P.L., were well on their way to the stile that led across the meadow. The Robins set off in hasty pursuit. The third Patrol, the Woodpeckers, evidently hadn't decided which stile was meant and were still arguing about it.

"We'll soon catch the Swallows up," said Sue.

"You may—I shan't!" complained Mandy, who

was small and found difficulty in keeping up with the others.

"Like a piggy-back?" asked the fourth member of the Robin Patrol, Anne, grinning.

The Swallows had disappeared by the time the Robins climbed the stile.

"This is an easy treasure-hunt," observed Sue. "The farm and the house near it are simple clues."

"We haven't finished yet," Kate reminded her. "Miss Page doesn't usually make things easy; she's pretty cute."

There was no sign of the Swallows when the Robins reached the crossroads, which they assumed was the place "where three roads meet."

"Where do we go from here?" asked Anne.

"The clue says 'Now just near here is quite a tease—Trace diamond necklace through the trees.'" Kate rubbed her chin. "I agree that it's quite a tease! What on earth is the diamond necklace we've got to trace?"

"Search me!" muttered Mandy.

"The Swallows must have solved the clue, as they aren't here," said Sue.

"Have they solved it correctly—that's the thing?" replied Kate. "What in the world can a diamond necklace through the trees be?"

"You said Miss Page doesn't make things easy," said Anne. "How right you were!"

Suddenly Mandy let out a cry and pointed. "I know what it is! Look what that car is doing!"

The Guides followed her pointing finger, and then Kate gave a cry. "Gosh, Mandy—well done! The 'diamond necklace' is the cat's-eyes."

Mandy nodded, and the others saw what Kate meant. The lights of the cars speeding along the road picked out the row of cat's-eyes in the centre of the road and illumined them so that they sparkled like diamonds.

"Clever girl, Mandy!" said Sue approvingly, thumping her on the back.

"I shan't solve another clue if you bash me on the back every time I do," Mandy told her.

"Come on—hurry!" urged Kate. "The Swallows must be miles ahead by now."

"The question is, though, whether they are miles ahead on the right track," remarked Anne. "They must be pretty smart to solve that 'diamond necklace' clue so quickly."

"I've got an idea that superior Linda is hot on treasure hunts," said Sue.

"I fancy she's got all her buttons on," admitted Kate.

The road with the cat's-eyes was provided with a footpath, so the Guides were able to walk alongside it safely. They went on for about half a mile, until the road began to slope steeply upwards.

"Doesn't the next clue say 'On steep hill rest awhile'?" asked Mandy hopefully.

"Yes, Mandy dear—but we've got to get to the top of the hill before we rest awhile—in other words, we've got to climb up it!" Sue laughed and put her arm through Mandy's to help her along.

They climbed the hill as quickly as they could. On either side of the road at the top there were tall trees, growing thickly together.

" 'Make your way down flowery aisle'." Kate read out the clue from her paper. "Can anybody see a flowery aisle?" she demanded.

"I'm baffled," admitted Anne.

"Me too," said Sue. "Come on, Mandy! What's the answer to this one?"

Mandy shook her head. "I don't know. I can't guess."

"Wait a minute," said Kate. "There's a gateway just a little way down. Perhaps that'll give us a lead."

She ran towards an opening bordered by two stone pillars overshadowed by trees, the others following. She peered at the nearest stone pillar and made out faded lettering: HILLTOP GRANGE.

They could make out faded lettering

Beyond the gateway was a long drive. It was overgrown and looked neglected, but the Guides saw in the dusk that it was bordered by unkempt masses of flowers.

"I say, d'you think this is the 'flowery aisle' down which we must make our way?" asked Kate.

"Could be. I wouldn't call it exactly an aisle, but I suppose we've got to allow Miss Page poetic licence!" said Sue.

"This is what she means all right," declared Mandy, excited now. "Lead on, Kate!"

"I suppose it is the place?" said Kate doubtfully. "I shouldn't think it's been occupied for years, by the look of it, and somehow I wouldn't have thought Miss Page would choose it for a treasure hunt."

"She's given to what you might call whimsy," Anne pointed out.

"I wouldn't call this whimsy!" declared Kate.

"Anyway, let's try it," urged Mandy. "There's nothing else like a 'flowery aisle' within sight, so far as I can see."

"And it's getting dusk," Sue pointed out.

"Very well." Kate led the way down the drive. "Keep together!"

They walked slowly down the long, dark drive.

"It's a bit creepy, isn't it?" whispered Anne.

Mandy nodded, without speaking.

At the end of the drive they came suddenly on a crumbling mansion, grey and ghostly in the falling dusk. Most of the windows at the front were broken, and the front door was missing.

"Creepier and creepier!" muttered Mandy.

"We'd better go in and look around," said Kate. "If the treasure's here we'll grab it and run. I don't fancy lingering here when darkness comes!"

Keeping close together, the girls entered the house. There was decay and decrepitude everywhere.

Suddenly a sound from somewhere in the great empty house startled them and brought them to a halt.

"W—what w—was it?" whispered Anne.

"It sounded like someone moving about in one of the rooms," said Kate. Then suddenly she laughed. "The Swallows!"

"You mean the Swallows have beaten us to it?" cried Sue. "They're here!"

"Come on!" cried Kate, suddenly bold.

She ran towards a door at the end of the hall from which the noise had come. It creaked open at her push. Then she fell back with a cry.

Suddenly a sound from the great empty house startled them and brought them to a halt

Facing her from the middle of the big room was a huge form, which moved back quickly as she stared at it. Then all the astonished girls heard a loud whinny.

"It's—it's a horse!" cried Sue.

"A pony!" shouted Anne.

"Would you believe it?" cried Mandy. "So this is the treasure! Our Miss Page has certainly done her stuff this time!"

Slowly Kate walked towards the pony, making soothing noises as she did so. The pony backed nervously away.

Mandy ran out of the house and tore up grass. After some coaxing the pony consented to take the grass from her hand.

"Well, now we've found the treasure we'd better take it back," said Sue. "I wonder where the Swallows got to?"

The pony seemed willing to be led from the room. Occasionally giving it grass, the girls were able to lead it out to the drive and then into the road. It walked quite happily between them as they made their way back to the Guide hall.

They were the last Patrol back and Miss Page was looking out of the door for them as they led the pony up to the hall.

"Wherever have you been?" demanded Miss Page. "I was getting anxious about you. And whatever is that you have there?"

"Why, the—the treasure from Hilltop Grange," Mandy replied anxiously.

"The pony," added Kate.

"The treasure—the pony?" Miss Page looked dazed. "The treasure was found a long time ago by the Swallows. It was in the church. It was the fruit, vegetables and flowers of the Harvest Festival to be brought here for distribution by our Guides to the old people of the village. Look!" She threw open the door of the hall and pointed to baskets of apples, carrots, swedes and other vegetables and flowers. "The Swallows won the treasure hunt in record time. I gather that Linda played a leading part in solving the clues; she's evidently quite expert at it."

"Then who does the pony belong to?" asked Kate, who, like the rest of the Robins, was looking very downcast.

"It belongs to me!" Linda, who had come to the door, ran suddenly out and flung her arms round the pony. "It's my dear Dapple! Oh, Dapple, I'd begun to think I'd never see you again!"

"Yours?" cried Kate. "But we found him at Hilltop Grange. He'd got himself right into one of the rooms."

"He's a scamp," returned Linda. "He's got a great big bump of curiosity, and it's always leading him into trouble. He's the nosiest pony in the world, but I love him, and I'm terribly grateful to you for finding him. He was missing all day yesterday, and I'd almost given up hope of finding him. He found a way of getting out of his paddock, and I was terribly afraid he might get on to the main road and be killed or injured. Thank you so very much for bringing him back."

"Well!" said Miss Page. "All's well that ends well, but I suggest, Robins, that next time we have a treasure hunt you don't jump to solutions so quickly. How in the world you got Hilltop Grange from my clue I can't guess. At the top of the hill you can see the church close by through the trees. The Swallows tumbled to it because of the reference to 'aisle' in 'flowery aisle'. Goodness knows what you thought a flowery aisle was!"

"We thought it was the drive to Hilltop Grange because it was lined with flowers," explained Kate.

"Well, I suppose it could have been," admitted Miss Page. "Anyway, it was a blessing, as things turned out, that you went off on the wrong track. If Linda's pony had got itself into a room at the Grange it might not have been able to get out again. I imagine the wind must have closed the door after it got in and imprisoned it. It might have been there for days or even weeks and even died."

The Robins felt very comforted by this. Linda was in no doubt about her feelings.

"I'd rather you misread all the clues than not get my dear Dapple back. I daren't think what he might have suffered if you hadn't found him."

The Robins were satisfied. The Swallows had beaten them to the treasure, but the Kingfishers apparently hadn't got beyond the 'diamond necklace', which had completely baffled them.

"We mayn't have got the real treasure," Kate told her Patrol, "but we brought back another one, much more valuable—Linda's pony."

"And we learnt a lesson," put in Mandy.

"What's that?"

"Not to jump to solutions!" grinned Mandy.

"BECOMING A HOMEMAKER" HINTS

To make use of milk cartons, flatten them and use them for fire-lighting.

Newspapers make excellent kindling. Roll them up and tie them in a knot. They're as good as dry wood for starting a fire.

A single thickness of newspaper damped on one side will act as a dustpan. Pat it down on to the hearth or floor, to which the damp side will stick while you sweep dust on to the top.

A good wad of newspaper is excellent for drying and polishing glass. Try it on window-panes after washing them or on the windscreens of cars you clean to raise funds for your Company.

For a quick repair to a jumper or other garment that you have caught on something and snagged, push the blunt end of a threaded needle from the wrong side to the right and into the tear. Place the end of the tear between the thread and needle, tighten threads and pull the needle back through. The tear will follow.

"SEASONS OF THE YEAR" PRESENTS

Lily Grose Shows You Interesting Things to Make

Springtime Presents

You will need yogurt pots, tile-fix cement powder, pretty seaside shells or small glassy pebbles which have been washed smooth by the sea, and clear varnish.

When you go on your first seaside outing or picnic, collect seaside shells. The best place to find them is at the seaweed-strewn tide-line. Perhaps you will find smooth, glassy pebbles in the sand or shingle. If so, you can use these treasures to decorate your plant-pot containers. Pot-containers are popular as presents, or you could make some for your sale-of-work stall.

Wash your shells and dry them in the open air to get rid of the strong salty smell. Wash and dry your glassy pebbles and wash and dry your yogurt pots.

Mix your cement powder with water. Use two tablespoons of powder and one tablespoon of water for each pot. Spread the mixture over the outside of your pot. Let the mixture on the pot harden a little (leave for about ten minutes), then arrange your shells and glass pebbles around the pot, pressing them firmly into your paste mixture.

Next day, when the paste has set, varnish the shells. The varnish will show up the pretty colours of the shells and make them look very attractive.

Summer Presents

Make a shoe-box aquarium to remind you of your seaside holiday.

You will need one shoe-box, thin card, blue cotton or fine elastic, fronds of dried

seaweed or brown and green strips of paper, small shells (washed and dried), sand, glue, white paper or spotted wall-paper and sticky tape.

Turn your shoe-box on to one of its long sides. Paint the inside of the top and the two sides blue. Paint the inside of the bottom of the box yellow. This will be the sandy bottom of your aquarium.

Cut out ten fish shapes in different sizes from your paper. Paint them different colours. When dry, glue them to the back of your aquarium. Glue the dried seaweed or your brown and green strips of paper between your fish.

Smear a little glue on the yellow bottom of the aquarium and sprinkle the sand on the glue. Then stick your small shells on the sand.

Cut out four larger fish shapes from the thin card. Paint both sides in bright colours.

Swimming Fish

When dry, make a hole with a pin through the top of each fish. Then make holes in the top of your aquarium. Thread cotton or elastic through the hole in the fish and tie securely. Pass the other end through the hole in the top of the aquarium and secure with sticky tape. The fish will move when there is a breeze blowing in your room and will appear to be swimming in their aquarium.

Autumn Gifts

In October make a Nature wall-plate.

You will need one paper plate, partly skeletonised sycamore "keys", dried leaf stems (for flower stems), small pressed dried leaves (press between heavy books), florets of a dried hydrangea head, dried montbretias or dried and pressed ferns, glue, and tape for a hanging loop for the back of your plate.

Dragonfly Borders

Arrange your flowers, leaves, leaf stems and ferns into a pretty bouquet in the centre of the plate. Glue into position.

Using four sycamore "keys" for wings, two short lengths of dried leaf stems for feelers, and a longer length for a tail, make dragon-flies and glue them around the edges of your plate.

Allow the glue to dry before you hang your picture up.

Winter Presents

Now make Christmas decorations.

For a pretty candle decoration for the table, you will need 1 cardboard tube from the inside of a paper-towel roll, 2 sections from a cardboard egg-box, 1 round silver-foil container from a small pie, yellow cotton-wool, white cotton-wool, and glue.

Glue the cardboard tube over one egg section. Glue the other to the other end of the tube to form the candle top. Pierce a hole in this top and push in a wisp of yellow cotton-wool for the flame. Secure with glue if necessary. Glue the other end inside the silver-foil container. Paint your cardboard candle red. Then glue some white cotton-wool around the top of the candle to cover the join where the tube meets the egg-container. Glue more cotton-wool down the sides of the candle as imitation candle-grease.

A Christmas-tree plant in a pot makes an attractive bedside decoration.

You will need 1 pine-cone to fit into the top of 1 yogurt pot, tile-fix cement powder, washed silver-top milk-bottle tops, glue or nail-varnish, and glitter dust.

Mix two tablespoons of cement powder with one tablespoon of water and spread the mixture around the outside of the yogurt pot. Press silver-foil milk-bottle tops into the cement to form a pattern round the pot.

Put a little cement near the bottom of the fir cone and push this into the top of the pot.

Brush glue or nail-varnish on the edges of the pine-cone, and before the glue dries sprinkle with glitter dust.

ANSWERS TO PUZZLES

WHICH WOOD? (pages 104/5): A–Chestnut, B–Ash, C–Holly, D–Birch, E–Yew, F–Larch, G–Hawthorn, H–Oak, I–Cherry, J–Wild Pear, K–Beech, L–Elm.   WHICH PATROLS? (pages 52, 70): Emma's–Snowdrop, Sally's–Thistle.

'INSECTIQUIZ' (page 81)

1. TRUE, but they are eggs and grubs for a long time.

2. FALSE. It has no sting and actually devours harmful insects like mosquitoes.

3. TRUE. It has eight legs and usually eight "simple" eyes.

4. TRUE. It has neither lungs nor voicebox, but chirps by rubbing its legs against its wing-cases.

5. FALSE. Its eyes are fixed, but bulge enough for it to see all round.

6. FALSE. The "veins" are merely a framework to stiffen the wings—like umbrella ribs.

7. TRUE. As in fish.

8. TRUE. The countless hairs on them vibrate to sounds.

9. FALSE. They have no teeth—only fleshy "lips" for sucking on the end of the proboscis (tongue).

10. FALSE. They keep the body in the nest until it crumbles to dust.

PICK THE FLOWERS (page 103)

1. SNAPDRAGON, 2. AZALEA (ZEAL), 3. LOBELIA (LOBE), 4. VIOLA, 5. IRIS, 6. ASTER (TEARS). The hidden flower is SALVIA.

THE CRAFTY KINGFISHERS (page 42)

GATE	DISH	TEA
MATE	SAW	STOVE
PATE	SAT	STOLE
PACE	CAT	STILE
PACK	CUT	CAMP
TENT	WOOD	CAME
BENT	FOOD	COME
BEAT	FORD	HOME
BOAT	FORE	BELL
MIST	FIRE	SELL
FIST	TIN	SEAL
FISH	TEN	PEAL

WHAT'S THE MESSAGE? (p.45)

ANSWER: Someone come and stir the pot. Or you will find you've burnt the lot!

"THE GIRL GUIDE ANNUAL"
DOUBLE-PRIZE COMPETITION

Owing to the large number of entries received, it was not possible to complete the checking in time to include the result of the competition in this annual.

The result, however, appeared in *Today's Guide* in the last week of June, 1972.